Wolf Signs

Talk about getting your signals crossed...

Robyn Maxwell doesn't care that her brother has to cancel out on their backcountry ski trip. She can do it alone. The fact she's deaf doesn't make her survival skills any weaker. The chance to get away from it all and relax in the Yukon wilderness is just what she's been craving.

Meeting wilderness guide Keil at the cabin starts cravings of another kind. Keil's one hot hunk of ripped, tasty male. Now she has to deal with raging hormones as well as strange questions about wolves and mates and challenges to the death.

Keil was trying for a nice reflective retreat before challenging for the Alpha position of his Alaskan pack. He wasn't planning on meeting the woman destined to be his mate, or finding out she's not aware she has the genes of a wolf.

Between dealing with his accident-prone younger brother, a deaf mate with an attitude and an impending duel to the death, his week—and his bed—is suddenly full.

Far from the relaxing getaway any of them had in mind...

Warning: Gives a whole new meaning to the phrase "talking with your hands". Includes dangerous use of sarcasm and hot nookie in a remote wilderness sauna.

Wolf Flight

An untriggered werewolf. A runaway Omega. It's not easy fighting destiny.

Tad Maxwell's workaholism serves to keep his bush-pilot company in the air, and his inner werewolf in check. In the two years since he discovered his heritage, he's resisted the longing to test the power of his wolf side. It would mean compromising his human principles.

Then Missy Leason re-enters his life. Ten years ago, their teenage attraction never went beyond hand-holding. Now their chemistry is off the charts, pushing him closer to the step he's not sure it's safe to take, especially with a human.

But Missy is more like Tad than he realizes. She's wolf too, and a wolf pack is a dangerous place to have secrets. Missy's Alpha has sniffed out her carefully hidden Omega powers. Her first response: run from the corrupt Alpha's plan to make her his mate. Step two: get to Tad, and hope like hell his untapped powers are strong enough to negate her own.

Every touch with Missy is hot, hot, hot, but even finding out she's pure wolf doesn't solve Tad's dilemma. Is she using him, or are they truly destined mates? Only one thing is certain. He will defend her to his last breath—on his terms. Even if it means losing his life.

Warning: Contains nasty Alphas, secret Omegas and werewolves acting raunchy on the dance floor. Sarcasm, wilderness cabins and hot nookie back by popular demand.

Look for these titles by

Vivian Arend

Now Available:

Granite Lake Wolves Series

Wolf Signs (Book 1)

Wolf Flight (Book 2)

Wolf Games (Book 3)

Forces of Nature Series

Tidal Wave (Book 1)

Pacific Passion Series

Stormchild (Book 1)

Turner Twins Series

Turn It On (Book 1)

Under the Northern Lights

Vivian Arend

A Samhain Publishing, Ltd. publication.

Samhain Publishing, Ltd.
577 Mulberry Street, Suite 1520
Macon, GA 31201
www.samhainpublishing.com

Under the Northern Lights
Print ISBN: 978-1-60504-794-2

Editing by Anne Scott
Cover by Angela Waters

Wolf Signs, ISBN 978-1-60504-476-7
First Samhain Publishing, Ltd. electronic publication: March 2009
Wolf Flight, ISBN 978-1-60504-683-9
First Samhain Publishing, Ltd. electronic publication: October 2009
First Samhain Publishing, Ltd. print publication: August 2010

Contents

Wolf Signs

Dedication

To My Sweetie,

We haven't quite traveled the world but we're on our way. Thanks for finding some awesome settings for us to explore. I'd like to write a couple of African adventures and maybe something set in New Zealand. You up for it? I love research.

Chapter One

6450 calories stared up at Robyn.

She adjusted the lid on the apple box to close it tight over the cheesecake and other food supplies. She let her gaze flow over the rest of the gear spread all over her apartment. Her pack, her skis, all of it gathered and ready to go for the annual trip with her brother to Granite Lake cabin.

A tight feeling of anxiety filled her as Tad made his announcement.

"I'm sorry, sis, but I have to take this request. Flying the climbing and research team to Mount Logan could end up being a regular booking. They're supposed to be working in Kluane National Park for the next five years, and if I can get on as their main pilot I'll be set." Tad reached out and slipped a loose strand of hair back behind his sister's ear. "I hate to cancel the trip on you—"

Robyn paced a few steps away before turning back to face him, her hands flowing smoothly as she spoke to her brother in American Sign Language. "I understand, Tad. You need to take the job. I'm still going to Granite."

"No way. You can't go by yourself."

"You have."

"But that's different, Robyn."

"Don't be a jerk. I don't have a penis so I can't go

backcountry alone?"

Tad raised his eyebrows. "It's not the lack of plumbing, sis, and you know it. I very seldom go bush alone and if I do meet anyone, it's not a big deal. I'm male, I'm strong and I'm not deaf. How do you plan on talking to strangers?"

Robyn threw a pillow his way before lifting her hands to sign at him. "I'll take some notepads. What are the chances of meeting anyone at Granite this time of year? We always go in February because no one else does. I'm packed, the food is packed, and I've got time off work from the bakery. You even booked a helicopter ride for me with your buddy Shaun. I've never gotten to fly in before.

"And wait a minute, what's with that little dig saying you're strong? Last time I checked I out-skied, out-wrestled and out-gambled your sorry butt, big brother, don't give me that as an excuse."

Tad narrowed his gaze at her. "Stop being stubborn."

"What? Waste all those years of training? You told me once to stand up for myself and do what I need to do, in spite of not being able to hear. Are you saying that doesn't apply anymore?"

"Of course not—"

"Good, because I'd hate to call you a hypocrite. I need to go to Granite. I need to get out of the city for a while. I'll be a good little girl and take the satellite phone along. I can check in with you Tuesday."

Tad ran a hand through his hair before collapsing on the couch in resignation. "Fine, you win. But if you need anything you call me or you call Shaun and he'll fly you out. Understand, Robyn? You don't have to do the ski if you don't want."

Robyn caught a glimpse of herself in the hall mirror. Shades of brown reflected back at her. Shoulder-length brown hair, big brown eyes with golden flecks, skin that always seemed to have a light tan for some strange reason, even after living her whole life in the Yukon. Her solid body was more than capable of doing the ten-mile ski. She'd been completing it with the family since she was nine years old. Tad had skied it with her and knew she loved every minute of the trip. She counted to twenty.

Slowly.

"Tad, are you looking for pain? Because I can kick your butt if you need it."

"What did I say?"

Robyn stomped up to him and glared into his face. Tad was her brother by adoption, and he and his parents were all darker in colouring than her. His short black hair stood in ragged spikes from his manhandling and his dark eyes stared back at her with confusion. "I like the ski across the lake. I like going into Granite cabin. I'm thrilled you got me the helicopter ride, but only because I want to take the ice auger to leave at the cabin.

"So don't expect me to be some kind of baby because you can't go with me this time."

Tad grabbed her hands and pulled her in for a hug. He let her step back so she could read his lips. "I was a bit condescending, wasn't I?"

Robyn nodded.

"Sorry. Hell, you've got a temper on you. Glad you didn't throw anything hard at me this time."

"I thought about it but my ice axe is already packed."

She turned to tuck away a few more items, picked up her backpack and placed it beside the door. He tugged on her arm to get her attention.

"You need some space, don't you? You seem really tense."

Robyn returned to her skis. She fiddled with the bindings for a bit before glancing back at Tad. "Yeah. Feels like the walls are closing in. I'll be okay if I can get some time away from the city."

"Robyn, there's something..." Tad hesitated, looking everywhere around the room except at her. He opened and closed his mouth a couple of times before shaking his head. "Never mind."

Robyn gave a heavy sigh. "Not again, Tad. You do this at least once a year. Whatever deep, dark secret you have I wish you'd spit it out. Or drop it and not get me curious. Are you gay?"

Tad sat back on his heels, his jaw dropping open. "Robyn!"

"Well, you seem to turn twenty shades of red every time you start this, I thought maybe it had to do with sex. I don't care if you are gay, you know. There's this great guy down at the bakery—"

"Thanks, but I'm not gay. It's nothing. Do you have your bear spray?"

Robyn blew her bangs off her face with a sudden snort and pointed to the pocket of her ski overalls. "Stupidest thing I've ever carried. I've never seen a bear, not once in all our trips."

"Someday you might be glad you have it, sis."

"But I could carry at least five more chocolate bars. That reminds me, you do realize if I gain weight this trip it's all your fault."

"What?"

"We packed an entire Mocha Chocolate Cheesecake to eat this week. Now I'm going to have to suffer through and eat the whole damn thing myself." Robyn licked her lips and grinned at him.

✧

The pilot pulled at her sleeve and pointed twice, left toward the lake and farther to the right behind the cabin.

Robyn shook her head and pointed to the left.

The lake.

The helicopter banked as he veered to change course. The surface snow around them stirred under the effects of the spinning props, and whiteness whirled away from the chopper until there was nothing but the solid snow base under the landing gear.

Robyn waited while the pilot trotted around to open her door. She helped unhook her skis from the landing blades while he removed the rest of her gear from the backseat and dropped it on the snow beside them. In under a minute she'd done a final check to be sure all her things were out, and giving the pilot a thumb's up, she crouched low and scrambled toward the shoreline. The wind buffeted her for a minute as the helicopter rose, lifting over the small hill to the north, returning to Haines Junction.

She looked around her and drew a long, slow breath, crisp air chilling the back of her throat. Not a cloud in the sky to block the blue. The mountains around her tall and snow covered. Beautiful and overpowering at the same time. The lake spread out before her, its large bay at her feet and the longer length of it stretching snakelike to the south to disappear around the bend of the mountain. A sense of home spread throughout her body.

Turning in a circle she noticed the cabin facing the lake had been fixed up since the last time she'd been out. Someone had repaired the front-porch supports and added a series of hooks along the north wall. Snow shovels and axes that had been buried under a good four feet of snow last February hung in plain sight, easy to access.

Continuing her visual scan, Robyn was surprised to see a new building a little ways down from the cabin. It was too small to be another sleeping area, and there shouldn't be a need for more storage here.

The temperature was warm for February, twenty-seven degrees, but the chill sank into her bones the longer she stood in one place. She trudged back through her footprints to ferry her gear to the cabin. The new building would be her treat to explore once she got set up for the night.

Soon her backpack rested on the low platform covering the back of the tiny one-room cabin. There was space for six sleeping bags to lie side by side, with an extra three-foot extension at their feet that was used as a bench. Robyn considered for a minute before placing her pack along the sidewall near the window. She doubted anyone else would show up at the cabin, but she'd better stake her claim just in case.

The second trip, she carried up the cardboard apple box filled with groceries. Because of the helicopter, the food this trip was different than her usual light dry goods. She had fresh fruit and veggies for at least four days, some nice French loaves, and the dreaded Mocha Chocolate Cheesecake. Flying in had some definite fringe benefits. She left the box on the small kitchen counter that ran along the left-hand wall up to the wood-burning stove. The cabin was so compact there was barely room left for a table and four chairs on the right side and a narrow bench beside the solid plank door.

Returning to the lake, she used the ice auger to cut a hole in the ice before carrying the tool up to the cabin and finding an empty hook to hang it on. Robyn grinned as she stared at it for a minute. She'd bought her contribution to the "leave it better than you found it" policy in a garage sale the previous summer for twenty bucks.

Lake trout for dinner. She could hardly wait.

But first she would check out the new addition to the area. Making her way through the knee-deep snow, she climbed up the last couple of steps that rose above the snow line, undid the locks and peeked in. There was a small open area with two windows and a snow-covered skylight overhead. Wood dowels lined the walls at head height with a low bench running around the wall space. Another door was set in the center of room.

Good heavens, was that a shower in the corner? Robyn walked to the enclosure in amazement. Someone had brought a shower stall up to Granite Lake and installed it in this small cabin. Her heart leapt for a second, wondering if her guess of what was in the other room was correct.

She hurried back, opened the central door and walked into the smell of cedar and wood smoke. In the corner was an old potbellied stove with river rocks piled all around it. Two levels of benches were built into the walls and a couple of large buckets graced the top of the stove.

A sauna. Someone had built a sauna.

She'd died and gone to heaven.

Tad was going to be pissed he'd missed this. But the real debate became whether she wanted get the fire going in here or if she should still go fishing for her dinner.

Robyn ran her hand over the smooth wood and breathed in the rich scent. Actually, it was an easy decision. She'd do both. Getting the fire going wasn't a big deal and she'd have time to fish before it warmed up properly.

The next hours passed quickly while Robyn set up her fishing line, laid out her camping mattress and sleeping bag, and got the two stoves going.

By six it was dark and Robyn lay flat on her back on one of

the upper benches in the now-toasty sauna. She had enjoyed pan-fried trout for dinner along with a glass of merlot, and she was on the edge of feeling very, very good. Her frustrations were slipping away with the sweat pouring off her body.

This was roughing it.

She sat up, scooped some more of the melting snow from the pot on the stove and poured it with care over the hot rocks to build up the steam in the room. Noticing the pot was close to empty she slipped out into the annex and pulled on her boots. Propping open the outside door Robyn walked into the darkness with a bucket in either hand.

And slammed into something solid that hadn't been there before. Something tall and hard and covered in...Gore-Tex?

Chapter Two

Spinning around TJ saw a naked woman, metal buckets flying from her hands as she bounced off him and fell backward. He reached to catch her before she could hit the snow and spoke calmly as she struggled frantically in his arms.

"Whoa now, settle down. I'm sorry I surprised you."

She continued to twist and scramble, one hand reaching down toward her boots. He wanted to release her but was afraid with how much she squirmed she would hurt herself. A sharp jab in the ribs made him gasp and loosen his grip. Another blow landed closer to his groin and his hands grew looser still.

"TJ, let her go, she's freaking out," Keil called from a short distance away and distracted, TJ dropped her. Suddenly he swore.

"What the... Damn it, put that away, you little hellion. I told you I'm not going to hurt you." He stepped back from where the woman crouched, a fixed-blade hunting knife extended between them as she scurried backward toward the safety of the sauna house. She slammed the door shut and they heard her dragging something heavy in front of it.

"What is going on? Hey, lady, we're not going to hurt you. We're just—"

"Stop." Keil joined him at the door. "There's something happening here that isn't normal. We surprised her but something else is wrong." He lifted his hand to touch the door, leaned forward and sniffed a couple of times, concern drawing his face tight.

TJ stopped as well and sniffed the air. "Oh shit, she's a wolf. Try and get away from pack for a few days and look what happens. It's like a conspiracy. Do ya think that someone out there has a spy camera keeping track of us when we leave Haines? That would be kinda cool if it was a hot group, you know, like the KGB, FBI, CSI, SEALs and all those letter guys. But not the SPCA or PETA. It would be scary having them on our ass."

TJ shuffled up to where his brother concentrated on scenting the air. He watched Keil lean his forehead against the door and close his eyes while continuing to draw long, slow breaths. Moving closer TJ sniffed again, hard. What was making Keil act so weird? He was like a kid in a candy store. Mr. In Charge, Super Wilderness Man, always totally with it and in control, sniffing like a dog after a long-buried bone.

Something was up, but for the life of him TJ couldn't figure out what. He shrugged and turned away, hitting his brother's arm as he moved, letting a wicked chuckle escape. "Of course, she was rather sweet. Think she'd be interested in—"

A violent push sent TJ flying backward into the snow.

"Hey, watch it!" TJ sat up in the waist-deep snow and brushed off his hands. A low menacing growl made him pause from his fussing. Glancing up he saw that Keil had begun to stalk toward him, eyes dark, teeth showing. The hair on the back of TJ's neck stood up, and he scrambled backward through the thick snow trying to keep a safe distance away.

"Damn it, what is wrong with you? I was joking around."

Keil paused. He dropped his head, and TJ watched his brother's body shake as he took some calming breaths. Long heartbeats later Keil's hand reached to help pull TJ to his feet.

They stared at each other before Keil turned back toward the sauna.

"Ummm, Keil, what's up? You look a little grey around the edges and that's not like you. I mean, there's a chick here. It won't be the quiet getaway we planned, but it's not like we ran into an Elvis-impersonator reunion. She's not going to be any trouble."

Keil choked out a laugh, a brittle, tight sound that made TJ take a cautionary step farther out of reach.

Just in case.

Finally dragging his gaze off the sauna door, Keil gave TJ a soft push on the shoulder toward the cabin. "We're going to have to write her a note or something to convince her it's safe to come out."

"Why don't we let her stay in there until the morning? She might feel safer venturing out in the daylight," TJ suggested as he started up the path.

"I'm not leaving her locked in there!"

"Hey, don't bite my head off, bro. I wasn't the one streaking in the moonlight. This time. And the only time I did try it those rotten twins, Rachel and Beth, stole my clothes and I had to climb in the back window of the pack house..." TJ's voice trickled away to nothing as he realized that Keil was still standing by the door. Shaking his head, he called in a singsong voice, "Helloooo. Earth to Keil. Hey, I thought we were going to write a note. What is the matter with you, man? You're acting like you've never seen a woman before and that's not true. You have the chicks all over you, all the time. In the pack and out of it. Not that you take advantage of your opportunities like I think you should. Leave her alone. She'll be fine. It's not like she's going to freeze or anything."

A loud snort followed him. "Look," Keil said, "I'm not

leaving my mate locked in a sauna all night because I was too stupid to figure out how to fix a misunderstanding."

TJ stopped in midstride. "Your mate?"

Keil sighed, his head turning to the sauna as if drawn to it. "Yup. I think so."

"Oh shit."

Robyn watched as the two men disappeared from sight and candlelight appeared in the windows of the cabin.

Well, that had been just peachy. *Great going, Robyn. Way to use your brains.* What a stupid, idiotic thing to do, walk outside in the buff without checking around first. She knew better than to assume people wouldn't show up. She hadn't even thought about animals, although right now she wished she had wandered up against a bear.

This was the kind of accident Tad had warned her about. Why he didn't like it when she did trips without him or their core group of friends. She was capable of taking care of herself in a survivor-type situation, but adding people to the mix always made it tough. The fact she was deaf kind of guaranteed that when meeting new people in the wilderness something was going to go screwy.

She dropped back on the sauna bench and tried to relax. She was still holding her knife, and twisting the handle in her palm, she rubbed the carvings with her fingertips like a worry stone. The familiar sensation calmed her to the point that she could begin to see the humour in the situation.

I bet they never expected to get flashed, she thought as she poured some of the now-hot water over her skin, cleaning off the sweat and rinsing down her hair. She wondered if the men would want the sauna once she was done. She wouldn't stock the stove, but leave a bed of coals.

Because she had to go back inside the cabin. It would be monumentally silly to spend the night in here just because she'd had a bit of a shock.

Besides, now they knew she had a big knife.

She toweled off in the sauna then dressed in the annex. A piece of white against the window caught her eye, and she lifted a candle up to examine it.

We apologize for frightening you. We are Keil and TJ from Haines, Alaska, and operate the wilderness excursion company Maximum Exposure. We are members of the Granite Lake pack. If you are afraid to come to the cabin, please put two candles in the window, and we will bring your sleeping gear and food/water to the door and you can retrieve it when you feel safe. But we promise you are safe to return. If you want, approach in wolf.

Robyn read the note with some puzzlement. Well, the first part was nice but what were they talking about "approach in wolf"? It must be some kind of backcountry code she hadn't picked up yet. They were from Haines, maybe it was an American slang. Sometimes the small differences between American and Canadian vocabularies caused weird things to happen.

Hanging her wet towel in the sauna, Robyn wrapped her hair in a dry one and faced the door. Squaring her shoulders she drew a deep breath. She could do this.

Walking toward the cabin she peered in the window, checking it out before approaching the door. One of the men sat on the edge of the sleeping platform, his face out of sight as he spoke, his hands wild as they swung in big circles.

Great, a waver. All that energy saying nothing.

The other leaned back against the table, his arms

supporting him, his gaze roaming around the room. Suddenly his eyes stopped and looked straight at her out the window. Even though she should be invisible to him, a person in the dark while he was in the light, he'd seen her. He stood a little straighter and lifting his arms, he crossed them over his heart and dipped his head.

Robyn stopped in shock.

That was the ASL sign for "love".

Robyn's last straw broke and she stomped the rest of the way up to the cabin and threw open the door. Dropping her things on the bench, she kicked off her boots and marched up to him and started the deaf equivalent of shouting with her hands and body in his personal space.

"You do not insult me like that. Asshole. I accept your apology for the mistake before, but you go too far. You are rude. What does...?" She pulled the paper she'd retrieved from the window and pointed to the line "approach in wolf". "What does this mean?" She stepped back and crossed her arms while she waited for his response.

The look on his face was priceless.

Confusion, complete and utter confusion.

Robyn spun toward the waver as he stood and she caught the last thing he said. "...using sign language?" She nodded, bicycling her hands in front of her while mouthing "sign language".

The larger of the two men made sure she was watching him before he spoke. "I'm sorry, I don't understand sign language. I think I've upset you and I didn't mean to. Is there a way we can talk?"

All the bluster drained out of Robyn like sand through a sieve. Typical. She came to get away from the drain of communicating with people and instead she was going to have to use extra energy.

Oh well, maybe they'd eat a few pieces of her cheesecake and save her the calories.

She held up a hand with a lifted finger, a signal she'd seen many hearing people use to ask for a minute. Going back to the door, she cleaned up her boots and went to her backpack, tucking away her gear and tidying up her hair. She turned to get a drink and found the man she'd yelled at standing with a glass in his hand.

"Would you like some water?" He offered it to her and she touched her fingers to her mouth then opened the hand toward him before accepting the glass. She drained it in one shot. Robyn grinned at the funny expression on his face as she returned the glass. It had been hot in the sauna, and she wasn't going to be ladylike and sip when she was thirsty.

He smiled back at her. Dark brown eyes, so dark they were almost black, twinkled at her.

"Would you like some more?"

She nodded and made a circle motion over her chest with her hand.

"Was that 'please'?" he asked.

Robyn gave him a reluctant smile. She nodded and sat at the table. There was something fascinating about the man, and she watched as he went to get her some more water. She'd placed snow-filled buckets here in the main cabin before her sauna, and the men knew the routine. They had one of the buckets on the side cupboard for cool water, and the other simmering on the stove to melt snow and keep the air moist.

She let her eyes wander over him as he added more snow to the hot bucket. He was big. One of the biggest men she'd ever seen, and perhaps rushing into the cabin and shouting at him hadn't been the smartest thing to do.

His dark brown hair hung in a braid almost to his hips. Broad shoulders covered with a dark T-shirt, he had a tribal tattoo that wrapped around his left arm at the biceps. She was tempted to move closer and examine it, but he returned with her full glass and she tried to hide the fact she'd been staring at him with a quick shift to face the table. She spotted the notepad and pencil she'd left out earlier. She tapped it and motioned for him to sit beside her.

You talk and I'll write. You need to make sure I see your face.

"I'm Keil and that's my brother, TJ."

Robyn Maxwell from Whitehorse.

"I'm sorry we frightened—"

Robyn interrupted him by waving a hand in the air and starting to write. *It was an accident. I couldn't hear you and I wasn't paying attention. Tell TJ I'm sorry I pulled my knife on him.*

Keil rotated around to face his brother. Robyn watched as TJ drew up a chair opposite her and held out his hand. "Nice to meet you, Robyn," he said drawing out his words in an exaggerated manner.

Oh goodie. TJ was an idiot. Robyn glared at him and shook his hand hard enough to make him pull back in surprise. She grabbed the pad.

I'm deaf, not stupid. Don't talk weird for my sake. She flipped the pad around to let him read it while she took another drink.

This was the hard way to get to know people. It was much easier when Tad was along, because she could talk to him and he'd pass on messages and it would end up feeling natural and not this ridiculous slow process. She sighed and grabbed the pad back. Keil laid a soft hand on her arm to get her attention and a curious sensation raced through her body.

Heat slid from his hand to her arm, tickling, tingling. What was that all about? She looked down at his hand and felt the warmth still radiating, small bursts of electricity racing up her arm and making the hair on the back of her neck stand up. He gave a slight squeeze to get her attention and she glanced at his face.

"What pack?"

She pulled back in confusion and shrugged.

"Robyn, you said you live in Whitehorse. Are you Takini or Miles Canyon pack?"

Here it was again. What was he talking about? It was too bad he seemed to be slightly crazy because he was the hottest thing on two legs she'd ever seen.

She hoped he was fun crazy and not kill-people-in-the-middle-of-the-night crazy. Writing a short note she tossed the pad toward him as she got up from the table. Putting on her coat, she took a final quick glance his direction before heading outside for a breath of air.

Yup, he was hot. Out of his mind, but very easy on the eyes. Smelt yummy too. She ignored the strange throbbing sensation in her limbs and forced herself to walk outside.

As the door closed behind her, Keil pulled the pad nearer and read it out loud to TJ.

"*Takini is a hot spring. Miles Canyon is where I canoe. A pack is what I carry my gear in. I don't know what you're talking about. I'm getting ready for bed. The sauna has coals if you want it. I will talk to you tomorrow. Good night.*"

"You think she really doesn't know she's a werewolf?" TJ asked.

"Why would she have any reason to pretend? I don't understand. She's full-blood wolf from what I smell."

"Me too."

Keil drummed his fingers on the table. She not only smelt like wolf, but another scent flowed from her that tickled the back of his brain and went straight to his cock.

The scent of his mate. The chemical trail that called his wolf to hers and would make them mates for life. He was pretty sure she was it, but until he got a taste of her skin when she was aroused he couldn't be positive.

Of course at the rate they were going, it would be summer before he'd get close enough to actually find out.

Grabbing clean clothes, the brothers made their way to the sauna. Thirty seconds after closing the door, Keil realized the sauna was a bad idea. Robyn's scent hung heavy in the closed space, sweet and spicy, filling his head with thoughts that were better not imagined while sitting naked in a small space with his brother.

"You know, she smells good."

Keil growled at TJ. "Shut it, pup."

"Well, she does. But, Keil, she smells good like 'Hey, Robyn, can you help me with this?' and not 'Hey, baby, can you help me? Wink, wink, nudge, nudge.' Know what I mean?"

"Please, spare me the Monty Python imitations."

TJ flicked some snow at his brother. "I'm trying to tell you something serious and you accuse me of imitating MP? I'm cut to the quick. For serious discussion I imitate political personalities. You know that."

Keil lay back on the bench and tried to ignore his younger brother. TJ was the most irritating, the most annoying...and the most observant person he knew. Leaning up on one elbow, he opened his eyes and cursed.

"Fine. Explain it. What are you trying to tell me and use small words. It's late and it's been a hell of a day."

TJ dropped to the lower bench and grabbed the cedar edging in front of him. "She smells good like I want to trust her and take care of her and I know she'll take care of me. She obviously affects you differently."

"Oh. How is that?"

TJ snorted as he pointed. "You've got wood from the smell of her left in a sauna, bro. You've got it bad and I bet she is your mate because you haven't even given her a proper sniff yet. I knew you were ready to be Alpha!"

Keil let his head flop back on the hard bench. TJ's leaps of logic were over the top. How he got from the fact Keil had a hard-on that could pound nails to making him Alpha was incredible.

"TJ, enough. Can we let this drop for tonight? The problem will still be there in the morning."

TJ's laugh was long and loud, and finally Keil joined in.

"Okay, bad choice of words. Don't point it out." Another howl rose from TJ and Keil gave up. He picked up the bucket of cool water and poured it over himself. He raised the other bucket.

"Want a rinse?"

When TJ nodded, Keil gave an evil grin and poured the contents of the half-snow-filled bucket over his brother's head. The icy-cold water streamed down and TJ's scream echoed in the small space.

Now Keil was ready for bed.

Chapter Three

Keil rolled over for the millionth time.

This was impossible.

He'd slept in a cave surrounded by soaking wet, stinking pack members when they'd gotten caught in a storm. He'd slept in a single hotel room with seven buddies on a road trip, all of them snoring loud enough to shake the walls. Both times he'd gotten more sleep than tonight.

All because of the small female body at the end of the platform.

He gave up pretending and sat up to admire her better. The moonlight pouring in the window showed parts of her and his night vision filled in the rest of the details. She was curled into a half-circle, one leg pulled up, her head resting on a pillow made from her extra clothes. She wasn't in the sleeping bag but under it, her body lying on a small soft blanket.

It was warm enough in the cabin that she'd shrugged off most of her coverings and his gaze slipped over her. He wished he could touch her with his hands. Her skin tone was lighter than his, her light brown hair escaping from the ponytail she'd made before crawling into bed. Keil stared, memorizing the curve of her cheek, the dimple just visible at the edge of her mouth. Her eyes closed in sleep had the longest lashes he'd ever seen.

He licked his lips. Looking at her made his mouth water. He was tempted to slide over and take her in his arms, nestle her against his body and—

Shit. He was hard again.

How could she not know about belonging to a pack? As a full-blood wolf, she would have had the ability to shift from human form to wolf starting around adolescence. While the werewolf genes were dormant in most half-breeds, full-blood wolves almost always had their genes triggered while still babies.

Robyn being deaf was unusual, but not a huge issue to him. He could learn to sign, if that's what it took. When she was in wolf form, they'd have no problem communicating since wolf was ninety percent sign language. As mates, they should be able to speak into each other's minds anyway.

And if he was going to challenge for Alpha, there was an even greater chance he'd be able to hear her thoughts. One of the perks of heading a pack was a strong mental link to every member. Add that to the mate bond and they'd be fine.

His mind slipped to pack problems even as his gaze continued to caress her body. The current Alpha and Beta were getting too old to be proper leaders. The Granite pack was large and more transient than most with the constant influx of newcomers from the Lower 48.

Every time a wolf got the itch to connect with their inner self, they seemed to make their way north, thinking that the wilds of Alaska would help them find themselves. All they found was that life required hard work, no matter were you lived. There was no easy ride anywhere, and perhaps even less here Up North.

Keil had begun to worry as more of their traditions fell away. It wasn't that he didn't like progress, but some things were tradition because it was good for the pack. Newcomers brought baggage with them, and a lot of what they were demanding the pack do to keep them comfortable went against everything the Granite pack stood for.

It was time for change. When the old leaders announced they would step aside and let someone younger take over, Keil knew it was his chance. He would have to slow down on his guiding business but having a strong pack would be worth it.

But he wasn't the only wolf with the potential to win the challenge. Another of the newcomers was Keil's equal in strength, but Jack's vision for the future of the pack traveled even further down the road to hell than the one they were on.

Keil groaned and rolled on his back. Finding his mate right now was going to make things difficult, to say the least. But was he sad he'd found her? Hell, no. Some wolves went their whole lives without discovering their mate. So he had a few issues to resolve.

Before next weekend. No rush.

A soft noise made him turn. Robyn was awake, pushed up on one elbow rubbing her hand over the side of her face and ear as if in pain. He scrambled closer, cautious not to frighten her, trying to be sure she saw him approach.

He mouthed the words to avoid waking TJ. "Are you okay?"

Tears were welling up in her eyes as she shook her head. She tried to sit and with little effort he lifted her, pulling her into his arms. He ended up rubbing his hand over the side of her head while he rocked her gently back and forth. She was tense at first but slowly relaxed, and his heart leapt. Keil wasn't sure what was going on, but she felt too marvelous pressed up against him to think it through. His fingers continued to smooth over her hair and cheek, the feel of her against him wonderful and right. Her skin was soft under his fingers, the warmth of her torso wrapping around him like a blanket.

And when Robyn turned her head in his hand and caressed it, he thought his heart would burst. He couldn't resist. Still cupping her face, he lowered his lips toward hers, brushing gently with a closed mouth, just to feel the friction of them coming together.

It was like a shock of electricity raced through her. She'd woken to the painful buzzing in her ear that was a sporadic occurrence over the years. It only seemed to happen when she camped with strangers, and she'd learned to deal with it by rubbing, hard, on the soft spot below her ear. But today at Keil's gentle touch, the pain receded, and a wonderful warmth built throughout her body like she'd never before experienced. As his lips touched hers something clicked within her and all she could think about was feeling him everywhere.

Oh, lordy, she wanted to be naked with him.

That was really, really not her.

She'd reached twenty-six years old with limited sexual experience. Whether it was because Tad was overprotective or because her deafness made her too unattractive to warrant more exploration, she'd never worried about it too much. She had read erotic stories over the years, and she knew how to climax, but she'd never had any desire to try much of anything with anyone.

Tad said she was saving herself for the "right man".

Her parents had told her that when it was time, she'd know.

After all these years she'd figured that the Timex took a licking somewhere along the line and busted, because no one had really turned her crank.

Until now.

This stranger made her mouth water, and she hadn't had a

real taste of him yet. She opened her lips a crack, to see what he'd do and his eager tongue slipped past to trace the edge of her teeth.

Damn, he tasted good.

A sudden rush of scent filled her head and made it spin. Tingles raced down her body coming to land between her legs. She reached out a hand to see if something was pushing on her crotch, but nothing was there except the internal pressure that made her want to squirm.

Keil's hand slipped around to the back of her neck, drawing her closer and shifting her mouth to a different angle as he continued to kiss her. She pressed into him, enjoying the pleasurable sensations flowing through her. Yet even as she kissed back she wondered what she was doing. Why she wasn't pulling her knife on him and getting him to back off?

He lifted her around to lie on top of him as his tongue worked its magic on her mouth. His heart beat under her hands, the long, hard length of his body warm against her torso and limbs.

And she realized the long, hard length of something else nestled between her legs. Oh. My. Word. She pushed up with her hands on his hard chest to stare into his dark brown eyes, uncertain what to do. She felt safe, even if this had to be the most insane thing she'd done in her life.

"Are you feeling better?" Keil mouthed as he traced a finger over the ear she'd been clutching moments earlier. Robyn nodded. "Let's get some more sleep. We'll talk this through in the morning, okay?"

She nodded, lowering her mouth to give him one more gentle kiss, before crawling off his body to rearrange her sleeping space. Any concern over her strange reaction to him was washed away by the quick relief of her earache.

She'd just straightened the bottom blanket when Keil's soft touch on her arm made her pause. His eyes were bewitching as he stared at her, silent for a moment.

"Please, can I hold you?"

Robyn swallowed hard. Oh man, did she want him to hold her. She nodded before ducking her chin down to avoid his eyes. He shifted his mattress closer, pulled her sleeping bag under them before wrapping an arm around her waist and drawing her back tight to his torso. Up against his warm and solid body. He pulled his sleeping bag over the two of them, nestled her head on his arm and wrapped his legs around hers, pinning her in place.

It was the most incredible feeling, safe and secure.

This was insane. She didn't know this man from Adam and here she was wrapped up like a jellyroll with him. His fingers slipped along her arm to link with hers as he rested their joined hands against her belly.

Yup, totally insane.

Robyn closed her eyes and fell asleep.

✧

Clattering pots and pans woke Keil in the morning and he groaned. There were times that being deaf would be a blessing. Or at least make him stop wanting to kill his brother. Wrapped up together in Robyn's warmth, he wasn't ready yet to get out of bed.

They had shifted while asleep and he was flat on his back with Robyn's head resting on his chest. Her hands clutched at him while one of her legs had slipped over his belly, the inside of her thigh pressing down on his morning hard-on. It was heaven and hell to feel the weight of her against him.

"So, I take it you've had an interesting night. It's obvious I sleep like a log. Want me to make coffee or do you want me to go ski for a few hours?" TJ's grinning face peered down at them, his eyes tracing over Robyn where she clung to his brother's body.

"Stop leering at her. Nothing happened. Yes, make coffee and stop being such a shit." Keil tried to speak softly but Robyn woke, reacting to the lifting of his chest. "TJ, go get breakfast. I don't want her to be any more embarrassed than she needs to be."

"What's to be embarrassed about? She's your mate. You could do the horizontal bop in front of the pack and no one would be embarrassed. Except Keith. He'd be embarrassed because he thinks he's got the biggest dick in the pack and if you..."

TJ's voice faded away as he dug into their food supplies for the coffee.

Keil sent up a prayer that Robyn wouldn't freak out when she found herself in his arms. He didn't want to move backward in their relationship. He sensed that today was going to be a big day. A day of big revelations. A day of—

"Ahhh." Keil slammed his mouth shut and reached down to grab Robyn's wrist. She'd slipped her leg off his cock when she started to wake, which was sad but understandable. But then she'd followed it by running her fingers over the hard length of him and finished by cupping his balls.

"You okay, Keil?" TJ wandered back with a worried expression on his face.

"Just fine. Um, leg cramp. Get the coffee."

"Yes, master. Right away, master."

Keil looked at Robyn who smiled at him, a mischievous glint in her eyes that he hadn't seen the day before.

She mouthed the words back to him, "Leg cramp," and squeezed. Her face was flushed but she was still smiling, and when she leaned up to kiss him, he thought he must have died and gone to heaven.

Whatever was happening, please don't let it stop.

Unfortunately after brushing her lips over his she pushed herself up, trailing her fingers over his torso in a maddening way before slipping from under the sleeping bag to go dress in her corner.

As he forced himself to ignore her, Keil watched TJ get out three cups and put on a big pan of ham steaks. A clothed Robyn came back into his line of vision and his brother stopped her.

"Good morning, Robyn. How do you say that in sign?"

Robyn paused. She flipped him a thumbs up, and placing her left hand by her right elbow, she lifted her right hand in an arc.

TJ copied her. "Oh, cool, like the sun rising. Hey, Keil, look," and TJ signed good morning to him.

A chuckle from Robyn made them both turn and regard her with amazement.

"You can laugh?" TJ asked.

Her smile fell away and Keil swore inside. She wrote a fast note and disappeared out the door. He checked to make sure she was just headed for the outhouse before reading the message.

I'm deaf, not mute. Lost hearing as a child. Virus. I have an ugly voice. Two sugars, please.

TJ gave a soft whistle. "Man, oh man, is she going to be a handful. I'm glad she's your mate and not mine. Did you two fuck—?"

Keil hit him. Not hard enough to do permanent damage but hard enough to make his eyes register the shock of it. After picking himself up off the floor, TJ carefully exposed his neck to his brother.

"You will use that brain of yours to remember to be polite when you speak to and of my mate. Understood?" Keil drawled the words as he poured the coffee and prepared Robyn's cup for her. "Even though it's none of your damn business if you were thinking straight you'd already know the answer. Use your bloody nose. No, we have not mated yet. Yet for some insane reason she let me kiss her and hold her, and while I'm pleased to report that yes, she's officially my mate, I have no idea why she doesn't seem to know a thing about wolves."

He sat at the table. "So I don't want you making any stupid remarks until we figure this out. Got it?"

TJ shrugged. "I'll behave. I figure it might be kinda freaky to be told something like 'Hey, didn't you know you're a werewolf and, oh, by the way, you're my mate. Oh, and there's going to be a challenge to the death next weekend for the leadership of our pack and I'm one of the headliners for the match.' I think telling it all upfront might be the easiest way." He turned back and flipped the ham. "Besides, there's nowhere for her to run while we're here. Gives you two time to work it out."

For the second time in as many days, the door behind them slammed open and Robyn charged in, her face red and her eyes blazing. She glared back forth between the two of them, her nostrils flaring slightly.

For not knowing she was a wolf, she had the evil-eye thing down pretty good, Keil thought as a shiver ran down his spine. He watched TJ struggle to keep his feet.

She surprised them by speaking. Her voice was gravelly and harsh but very powerful. Keil had heard a few Alphas over the years and she ranked up there with the best of them.

"Who is my mate?"

Like a flash TJ pointed to Keil. "Crap, has she got my number. I hope she doesn't tell me to go jump off a bridge or something because I—"

Robyn stormed up and grabbed the pad of paper. Keil read over her shoulder as she wrote.

If you don't want to be overheard don't talk where a lip reader can see you.

Werewolf?

Mate.

Challenge. To death.

What the HELL are you talking about?

She pulled away from the table but stopped to add, *Where is my coffee? And it had better be strong.*

Chapter Four

It took three hours, two pads of paper and fourteen fried ham-and-egg sandwiches. Keil thought that on the whole it went pretty well, especially since he'd managed to not to skin TJ alive during the interrogation.

Robyn stood stiff and angry at first, looking ready to throw her coffee cup at them if they made one wrong move.

"Come, sit down and we'll explain everything." Keil pulled back a chair for her and she sat warily, shifting to keep both of them in her sight.

"Sorry, bro, guess my mouth got us both in trouble this time." TJ lightly touched Keil's arm in apology. A sudden rumble of the floorboards made them both swing to look at Robyn as she stomped her feet and glared at them. She pointed to the chairs and wrote rapidly, breaking the pencil lead as she underlined her final word.

I will talk this out with you. Sit down and don't you dare speak again when I can't see you. Ass.

Keil held out a reassuring hand and sat, motioning for TJ to join them. "I understand. We'll answer your questions. What do you want to know?"

Robyn found another pencil and opened to a new page. *Don't think because I went a little crazy last night and let you touch me you can jerk me around this morning. You're insane, right? Escaped from some home?*

"No, Robyn, it's true. We're able to turn into wolves."

Prove it. She leaned back in her chair and stared at them mockingly.

The two men exchanged glances.

What? You need a full moon?

Both men dropped their heads into their hands for a moment. Bloody fairy tales. Finally Keil looked up to see Robyn's very confused expression.

"No. We don't need a full moon. We also don't bite people to turn them into werewolves. You either have the genes or you don't. Sorry, that's one of those tall tales that drives us crazy. We'll have to, umm, take off our clothes to change." Keil watched Robyn's face turn white. A blush rose to colour her cheeks and her eyes brightened with the mischief he'd seen earlier in the morning. Good, maybe this wouldn't take too much damage control.

She flipped the pad across the table. *A private strip show? Goodie. Even if you don't turn into anything the morning isn't a complete write-off.*

Keil laughed and turned to TJ.

"You should be the one, Keil, she's gonna see you naked the most often."

Keil glared at his brother.

"What? You still having problems with that boner? Man, now I really think you should shift. It would serve you right for hauling me along on your retreat instead of letting me go hang out at Klondyke Kate's with the rest of the pack."

"TJ."

"All right, don't get your fur in a knot. I'll shift, but you keep an eye on her. If she signs anything that looks like 'cute doggy' or 'sweet fluffy wuffy', I want to learn them to insult the boys at the next pack meeting."

Robyn raised her eyebrow.

"Stop it with the Spock look, Robyn, that seriously freaks me out. I keep expecting to see you grow pointy ears and hear you announce, 'But this is not logical.'" TJ continued rambling as he dropped his clothes and stood naked in the middle of the cabin. He waggled his eyebrows at her and she blushed.

"Get on with it before I apply the Vulcan death grip to you, little brother." Keil spoke through clenched teeth.

TJ shimmered and there were two images overlapping each other, another shimmer and there was a large silver grey wolf sitting on its haunches in front of them. Robyn tensed. Keil watched her rise from the chair, eyes wide with wonder. She stood for the longest time and simply stared, her breathing rapid, face flushed. He was ready to take her arm to reassure her when she dropped to her knees and reached out in slow motion to brush the fur on TJ's head and neck.

After a few strokes of her hand, TJ rolled over to his back and tilted his neck up. A surge of pleasure raced through Keil's veins at the sight. His brother, while not always the sharpest knife in the drawer, was a physically strong wolf. TJ didn't give instant obeisance to just anyone. Another indicator that the woman kneeling by Keil's feet was going to be a powerful addition in his life.

TJ shifted back and Robyn was caught stroking her hand down his naked chest.

"Damn!" Robyn shouted and shot away from TJ, backing into the door.

"Oops, sorry, Robyn. You were tickling me something fierce. Boy, am I glad you didn't say 'shit' or some other swear word like that. With how strong your voice is I'd have been in a hell of a mess," TJ muttered quietly to himself as he pulled on his clothes.

Keil watched as Robyn closed her eyes for a moment and drew a shaky breath. Hell, could TJ do anything without screwing it up?

Keil refilled her coffee cup and waited for her to open her eyes. He patted the seat next to him. He wanted to pat his lap and have her crawl into it like last night. Actually, he wanted to strip her down and crawl into her, but that was going to take a little more time and patience on his part.

Hell, he hated being patient.

Her head was spinning, her heart beat a million times a minute and somewhere along the line she must have fallen down a rabbit hole.

Tad was never going to believe this. She was having trouble believing it and she'd seen TJ change, she'd touched his wolf form. It wasn't an illusion.

Unless there'd been something in her coffee. She gave it a cautious sniff. Smelt like normal Midnight Sun brew. She glanced up to see Keil's gorgeous eyes watching her. A shiver raced down her spine and heat flared in her belly.

Damn, he was potent.

She grabbed the notepad and sat for a bit thinking what to write. She twisted her face up, tapped the pencil a few times while biting her lip. Finally she went for honest.

Well. I'll admit it. That was pretty cool.

Keil smiled at her and she melted some more. Between his smile and the expression in his eyes, moisture was pooling in her mouth. And farther south.

She took a quick sip of her coffee and dragged her eyes

away from his.

So what makes you think I'm a wolf? I've never turned into anything.

"You smell like wolf." TJ leaned forward in his chair and sniffed in her direction. "Yup. I can't explain it better than that. I can't have you sniff a human and then sniff a wolf 'cause, we're all wolves here. But when we go back to civilization, we can show you. Well, even there it's tough to explain to someone that you need to sniff them but don't want to say why. Trust us. You're a wolf."

Keil nodded in agreement and Robyn shifted in her chair to stare out the window. A tidal wave of emotions swept over her. The ability to turn into a wolf. Who wouldn't want to be able to do that? It was the stuff of fairy tales and escape literature everywhere.

It also called to something deep inside her that had felt cooped up and trapped for many years. While she enjoyed her job at the bakery, and she loved her brother, she was never completely happy unless she was somewhere out in nature—skiing or hiking or canoeing.

Maybe this was the reason.

Robyn pushed the notepad at TJ. *How come I've never turned furry?*

TJ wrinkled up his nose and considered for a minute. "Keil? Ideas?"

Keil's hand stroked down her arm and she bit back a moan. Oh man, that felt good. Her skin itched to be touched, and as much as she needed to find answers, she needed to jump Keil more. The attraction that had begun last night, causing her to lose all sense and sleep in the man's arms, it seemed to be growing.

Concentrate. She needed to concentrate on the cool idea

that she might actually be able to turn into a wolf.

"Robyn," Keil said. "Full-blood wolves like us are born with the genes to be able to shift, but they're turned off in newborns until triggered. Kind of like they're dormant. For some reason your genes must have never been switched on."

A trigger?

Keil nodded. "Yeah. It's a hormone and newborns get it from their mom's milk."

Robyn's stomach fell. It more than fell, it leapt off the edge of Mount Logan and plummeted into the depths of the nearest crevasse.

The possibility that she was a magical being had excited her. Seeing TJ change had woken something inside her, full of joy and freedom, and a deep happiness she'd been missing all her life. Now it was slipping out of her reach and there was nothing she could do to stop it. She pushed away from the table and grabbed her coat, fighting back the tears as she rushed outside. She saw Keil rise to his feet, but she ignored his outstretched hand.

Damn, it wasn't fair.

She managed to get her coat done up before the tears fell. She stood gazing over the lake, arms wrapped tightly around her torso as her eyes welled up and overflowed. The bright sunshine around her did nothing to lighten the spot of darkness she felt at the loss of something she'd wanted. Something she hadn't realized she'd wanted so much.

Robyn felt him approaching. Gentle arms slipped around her torso and pulled her back into his body, supporting her. Holding her loose enough she could escape if she wanted, but close enough to let her feel his concern.

Another sob escaped before she could stop it, and Keil turned her and gathered her up against him like she was a child. She wrapped her arms around his neck, buried her face in his coat and let the misery release.

Her heart hurt.

Slowly, feeling his strength, feeling the comfort he offered, the pain eased. Keil's hand ran over her hair, and she remembered him touching her like that last night. He must think she was some kind of emotional yo-yo, running hot then cold. She took a deep breath and sniffed hard, pulling away from his embrace.

Keil reached a hand to cup her face. He wiped away a tear with his thumb. "I'm not sure what's wrong, but I think I've guessed a bit. Did something happen to your mom when you were born?"

Robyn nodded. She patted her pockets searching for tissue when Keil handed her a clean hankie. It took a minute to get herself back together, Keil politely ignoring her runny nose and wet face until she felt presentable.

She flicked glances up at him as he stood waiting for her. He gazed over the lake, his strong body like a pillar of granite. What was it about this man that fascinated her? He turned to see if she was ready and held a hand to her. Robyn grasped his warm fingers, enjoying the tingling sensation that raced up her arm as he wrapped his hand around hers and led her back into the cabin.

Inside Keil refused to talk. Instead he made her up a plate of food and sat beside her while he ate his own meal. The lump in her throat settled, aided by the fact that sitting in close proximity to Keil made her mouth water and she had to swallow twice as often as usual.

TJ spoke while he ate, which made for confusing moments as Robyn misread most of what he said. He was telling her all about their pack and how they spent time together in human form as well as in wolf. At one point she was sure that he said something about mooning people down main-street Haines, but that had to have been the extra large piece of sandwich he'd shoved in his mouth.

Breakfast finished, Robyn had to admit she felt a bit better. Having an emotional breakdown on an empty stomach was too much. Keil grabbed her dishes and kissed her softly on the cheek. "We'll wash up, you write. Tell me what's got you worried."

His dark eyes stayed on her until she nodded, then he turned away and got to work. He and TJ goofed off with the dishtowels and soap bubbles while they cleaned up the dishes and tidied the sleeping bags. Robyn sipped at her coffee as she watched, the love between the brothers clear.

She forced herself to pull the pad closer and write. When she finished she found Keil staring at her from where he sat waiting on the edge of the sleeping platform. His gaze ran over her body and he wasn't trying to hide the look of desire on his face. Their eyes met, and the shock of connection thrilled through her.

The wolf thing. It had to be something to do with animal attraction that was making her want to roll all over the floor with the man. Preferably naked. She licked her lips involuntarily, and the answering flash in Keil's eyes heated her blood to near boiling.

Damn, it was time to stop with the coffee and break out the ice water.

Keil tapped the space next to him and held out a hand for the notepad. "Come here, Robyn, sit by me while I read." She glanced over at TJ who was sprawled in a chair in front of the stove, making notes in the cabin's journal, before she took a step toward Keil. "He's going to let us talk this out alone."

Robyn sat, highly aware of the feel of his thigh touching hers as he shifted his body to wrap an arm around her torso and snuggle her tightly to his side. If she looked up she could still see his lips move.

In fact his lips were close enough to kiss if she leaned forward a tiny bit.

She whipped her head back to safety, examining the notepad and the message she'd written.

I was told that my mother and father were hunting caribou along the Dempster Highway when there was an accident at their hunting camp. Someone's gun went off and the bullet killed my father instantly and wounded my mother sending her into shock. The others at the camp managed to get her to the hospital at Dawson City where I arrived almost two months early. When my mother died right after my delivery I was adopted. All I have from my parents is my boot knife.

I guess that's why I never got "triggered"? I can't turn into a wolf.

I wish I could. I bet it's amazing.

She glanced up to see if he'd finished reading. He smiled down tenderly. "It's going to be all right. I'll explain a couple things first to help you understand."

He ripped off the top sheet of the notepad to a clean page. She watched over his arm as he divided the page in three parts and drew a circle in each part. In the top circle he wrote *Full-blood*, in the bottom he wrote *Half-blood*. He left the middle one empty. He adjusted them both to sit comfortably on the platform and face her better.

"Short biology lesson, Robyn. Full-blood werewolf, both Mom and Dad have the genes. Pass the dormant gene to baby. Baby triggered with hormones in milk, can turn to wolf around puberty." He lowered the notepad for a moment. "And if you think that teenage humans are moody, wait until you see an angst-ridden fifteen-year-old wolf. Very scary."

She snorted at him, and he winked and continued.

"Half-blood, only one parent has wolf genes. They're still passed on to the baby, dormant, but for some reason even milk from a werewolf mom won't trigger them. The hormones have to come from something else." Robyn watched as Keil wrote *milk* across from the top circle. He paused before writing *sex* across from the bottom circle.

"Half-blood wolves can get triggered by having sex with a full-blood. The hormones released during unprotected sex work fast, and since wolves can't get STDs, it's both effective and safe. There's a little added complication for males because of something called 'FirstMate', but females don't have to worry about it." He stopped and Robyn swallowed hard.

Well. That was a bit of a surprise.

One circle left to fill in. She watched as he wrote her name in the empty space.

Oh shit. She knew where this was going.

She grabbed the pen and flipped over the page, crawling away from him on the platform to write. She might have the hots for the man. No way was he going to use a biology lesson to get into her pants.

You want to have sex with me?

The flash of hot desire in his eyes answered the question faster than his mouth could.

"Hang on, Robyn. There's one more thing I need to explain. And that's all I'm doing, explaining. You get to make any decisions you want based on what I tell you. Trust me."

Robyn hesitated and then insistently shook the notepad at him. If he didn't 'fess up she was going to hit him.

"Hell, yes, I want to make love with you. But that's because you're my mate."

Robyn's fingers were awkward as she scrambled to respond. *Convenient. Maybe I should ask TJ if he wants to fuck me too.*

Keil burst with a roar that she felt down to her bones. "No one else is going to fuck you, especially not TJ!"

Out of the corner of her eye she saw TJ fly backward off his chair to land in a puddle on the floor. "Holy crap, Keil, what are you telling her?"

TJ must not have liked how Keil answered because he cowered lower on the floor. "Well, hurry it up, listening to one side of your conversation is scaring me to death."

Robyn considered for a moment and held up her hand to Keil. She snuck over to TJ and wrote him a note. Even if they'd rehearsed this, she didn't think TJ was fast enough to try and pull one over on her. He'd be forced to tell her the truth.

Keil says he's my mate. What does that mean and how can I tell if it's true?

"Hey, bro, she's asking me about you."

Robyn stepped back toward the sleeping platform keeping her eyes firmly on TJ.

"Of course I won't touch her. First, promise you won't hurt me."

TJ crawled off the ground. He wrinkled up his face and gazed upward as he rubbed a finger over his lips, as if trying to remember something. Shortly he nodded to himself and turned to face both Robyn and Keil.

"Okey dokey. Mates are like getting married, only better for five reasons." He held up a hand and lifted a finger with each comment he made. "First, mates have similar interests and tastes. Second, the chemical attraction between mates makes it impossible to miss knowing they are 'the one'. Third, sex between mates is super hot and stays that way for their entire lives. Fourth, mates are connected deeper than physically, there's a mental and emotional connection too. And finally, mates never, ever fool around on each other." TJ looked at Keil who stood with his mouth dropped open in amazement. "Pretty good, hey, Keil? Tony and I wrote that up for the pack chicks when they wanted to do a wolf version of a Cosmo 'Find Your Perfect Mate' quiz."

TJ grabbed Robyn by the hand and pulled her with him as he went to stand next to Keil. "How you can tell it's true is easy. Remember, bro, you said you wouldn't hurt me. Robyn, give me a kiss."

"TJ."

"Just on the cheek! Check out my scent and how it makes you feel. Then kiss Keil. That'll explain better than words." He turned his face to the side, keeping a wary eye on his brother.

Robyn bit her lip. She didn't need to do this "test" of TJ's, she knew what he was saying already. She knew she was sexually attracted to Keil. Completely and utterly attracted.

But doing the test meant she could kiss Keil again.

She leaned toward TJ and took a long breath in through her nose. Nothing but the smell of dish soap and the slightly earthy scent of a male missing his morning shower. She touched his cheek with her lips and felt like she did when she kissed Tad.

Connected, like family. No fireworks.

She shifted her weight and stared up into Keil's beautiful eyes. She started to take a deep breath but stopped quickly. His scent filled her. She could taste him, feel him slip down into her lungs and throughout her whole body. He smelt like the air of a starlit night, and dark-chocolate fondue and raw, passionate sex. Unable to stop herself, she ignored his offered cheek and grasped him by the hair, pulling him down to her reach so she could clasp their mouths together. As Keil reacted, their tongues tangling together, Robyn acknowledged that she'd never felt anything like the satisfaction she experienced at every contact with the big man in front of her.

Well, it seemed she was getting hitched.

Chapter Five

"This doesn't mean we'll do anything until you're ready," Keil said when he finally managed to drag himself away from Robyn. "We can take our time, get to know each other first. Now that I've found you, I can wait."

Her bright eyes shone back at him.

TJ bumped up from behind.

"Umm, Keil, but what about—"

Keil swung his elbow and connected with TJ's gut.

"Ugh." The air whooshed out of TJ, but he struggled on. "I'm just saying—"

Keil turned to face his brother, careful to hold Robyn close enough that she couldn't read his lips. "No, you're not saying another word about this. Understand?" It was a command, said in a tone that TJ couldn't ignore. Robyn wasn't the only one with the Alpha voice.

TJ froze. He dropped his eyes. "Understood."

Keil pushed Robyn away a bit and winked at her. "It's been a tough morning and I think we could use some exercise. Ski to the top of the pass for lunch?"

She nodded with enthusiasm and slipped away to change.

Keil wanted to give her some time alone to think about everything she'd learned, but his wolf refused to let her head out unprotected. Split personalities were tough to deal with at the best of times, and right now, Keil's wolf was pissed. It didn't see what the problem was and why there was no marking and mating happening.

Me too, bud, Keil thought.

He let his eyes trace over Robyn's hips as she tucked in her long-sleeved undershirt. In his mind he could already feel the weight of her body slipping over his shaft as he held onto those hips and helped her ride him. His aching cock pressed up against his ski pants and he had to adjust himself.

Again.

Yup, he was all for making the sacrifice to help her be able to shift to wolf.

Part of him wanted to send TJ back to civilization ahead of time, giving them some privacy. Only with the way TJ skied, he couldn't be left alone. The boy would probably get lost, or break a ski, or have some other disaster.

Damn. Trapped in the bush with his mate and an unwanted chaperone.

No, it was for the best. He needed to give Robyn time to adjust. Time to talk to her family and be able to accept the changes that would take place if she triggered her wolf. It wouldn't be fair either to make her full wolf and his mate if he died in the challenge on Sunday. It would be far better to wait until after the weekend when he'd have the proper time and energy to court her.

Even if it made every cell in his body scream in protest at the thought of waiting.

He watched as Robyn removed three avalanche monitors from the shelf and set them to the same frequency, checking the blinking lights to be sure they worked.

"No way, Keil. Oh man, you know I hate wearing those

things. Tell her I don't have to," TJ whined.

Robyn held out the devices to the men, her eyebrow rising at the sight of TJ pulling back and hiding his hands behind his back.

"I hate them."

Robyn's shrug said she didn't care what he thought as she stepped up to him, slipped the strap over his neck and fastened the waist belt. She reached up and patted TJ's pouting cheek while she batted her eyes and gave him an evil grin.

"I feel like a dog with a collar."

Robyn snorted and turned to make sure Keil wore his monitor correctly.

"I do this for a living, Robyn, you'll get no complaints from me." Keil reached and adjusted the straps around her waist, unkinking a section of elastic to make it lie flat against her body.

His fingers traced along the straps stretching over her torso, and his heartbeat increased at the feel of her under his hands. He looked up and saw her watching him. She swallowed hard, and her tongue darted out to moisten her bottom lip.

"It'll feel better if it's even under your coat." Keil's hands paused for a moment touching the tops of her hipbones. She was halfway into the embrace of his arms, and he wanted nothing more than to complete the move and pull her to him. To feel her pressed along his whole torso. To lower his mouth to hers and taste her.

She shifted as he leaned closer, temptation pulling him, her eyes drawing him like a magnet. Closer her mouth came as he reached farther around her body with his hands to caress over her back.

A sudden sharp pain shot through his left buttock, shoving him hard into Robyn's body as they careened backward toward the table.

"What the—?" Keil roared as he grasped Robyn and swung her around to avoid crushing her.

Behind them TJ threw gear left and right as he dug through his pack. His ski poles were tucked under his arm, extended backward, and every move he made shot the pointed tips in their direction.

"You bloody fool!" Keil attempted to grab the moving poles but they kept dancing out of reach. A sudden extra enthusiastic twist by TJ forced the poles hard toward them.

Keil pushed Robyn to the side as he shouted, "TJ, freeze!"

The solid *thunk* of the ski tip spearing into the wood table finally pulled TJ away from his rummaging to look closer at them.

Robyn and Keil stood side by side, the ski pole quivering as it jutted into the room from between their hips. TJ's innocent expression was beyond irritating.

"What?"

"TJ, you're a menace to everyone around you." Keil growled as he yanked the offending pole out and held it to his brother.

"How did that get there?"

Keil twisted toward Robyn and, placing a hand on her shoulder, made sure she could see his lips move.

"Is there an appropriate sign to tell my younger brother that he's a shithead and if he doesn't watch it, I'll tie him to the outhouse with a short leash?"

Robyn made a show of turning to face TJ and shaking her arms. Then she slowly raised her hand and flipped TJ her middle finger.

"Yeah," Keil said, "I thought that should about cover it."

✧

They skied single file down the lake, Robyn following Keil as he broke trail. He insisted on going first and Robyn fought back a laugh. He was very much like Tad, refusing to let anyone work harder than him.

Still, it gave her time to let her mind wander as she simply followed the ridges he left in the snow. While everything she'd been told this morning seemed to be impossible, the proof of TJ's change into his wolf form made it clear that this wasn't some practical joke they were trying to pull on her.

There was also the matter of her instant attraction to the large male striding in front of her. Robyn lifted her gaze to watch him ski, efficient as he worked to make tracks in the foot of soft snow that lay on the surface of the frozen lake. Something about him fascinated her.

Like a deer in the headlights of a fast-approaching truck, she was waiting for the impact to knock her silly.

The pheromones between the two of them were cooking hot. Before the little ski-pole incident, she thought she was going to end up as a snack. Heck, she'd wanted to be nibbled on. Tingles ran all over her body even thinking about Keil and his touch. The way she'd been wrapped up around him when she woke this morning, the reaction of his body to her touch. The strange way he was able to comfort her in the middle of the night. The usual repercussions from an earache would have her moving slow for the whole day, with a nagging headache to boot. One touch of his hand, a little cuddle, and the pain had drained away.

They were like a stick of dynamite and a Bic lighter. Too much more time together and something was going to blow.

She sighed as she wished for the hundredth time that Tad

were here to bounce ideas off. Her brother. Was he a wolf too? He'd never said anything. If this was news to him, was he going to be surprised.

Of course if he already knew she might have to kill him.

She could already hear him complain about her acting irresponsibly and doing this trip alone. Tad always said she was going to end up meeting some strange wackos in the backcountry. He probably hadn't thought she'd meet someone who wanted to turn her into a werewolf.

As they approached the bottom of the pass, Keil stopped and dropped his daypack. Robyn joined him and the two spent a moment enjoying the view, the sunshine on the snow, the mountains rising boldly around them. Keil nudged her arm, passing his water bottle after taking a long drink. Robyn saw him lick a drop of water left on his lip and a warm buzz shot through her. There was something erotic about sharing a water bottle that she'd never noticed before in any previous backcountry trip.

Robyn took a sip, very aware of Keil's eyes watching her mouth, watching her throat move as she swallowed. She lowered the bottle slowly and smiled at him. This courting business was going to be fun.

"I'll head uphill. Wait for TJ and make sure that he takes a drink. He's known for getting dehydrated. Okay?" He brushed his fingers over her lips in a gentle caress before turning away.

Robyn stared as Keil traveled smoothly up the hill on an angle, his powerful body setting the difficult trail with seeming ease.

Wow. Mates with Mr. Studmuffin. How did she get so lucky?

Only there was trouble in paradise. Something had happened this morning right before they set out. TJ was upset and he'd been fine until Keil had cut him off.

She was going to find out why.

It took a few minutes for TJ to catch up. Robyn handed him the water bottle, holding it second longer than necessary to force him to take a close look at her. When she was sure that he was watching, she motioned toward Keil with her head. She tapped her fingers together like they were lips speaking.

TJ bit his lip. "Ah, man, this is unfair. Keil told me to stay quiet. You gotta understand, as a human, he's my brother and I feel loyalty to him. He's also the most powerful wolf I know, and it actually hurts to think about disobeying him."

Robyn pointed to Keil and herself followed by linking her fingers together.

"Yeah, I know you guys are gonna be joined as mates. That means you're strong enough that it hurts to think about disobeying you too." He tilted his head to the side and with a pained expression asked, "I don't suppose I can talk you into letting me off the hook?"

Robyn felt guilty for pushing him, but there was something here that she needed to know.

She spoke out loud. Soft but clear.

"Tell me."

"Arghhhhh! Damn. Fine, I'll spill. Keil didn't tell you the whole truth about mates. It's not something you can put off that easy. He's trying to give you time to adjust to the whole idea of being a wolf and all that. He's being noble." TJ stared up the hillside where Keil was making the first switchback. "Keil is going to challenge for the leadership of our pack on Sunday. He's way stronger than the other guy, and I know Keil can win.

"Only the challenge is in both human and wolf form, and it can get a little messy, especially if either challenger's wolf isn't under control.

"The longer you and Keil wait to finish mating, the more distracted his wolf is going to get. I'm not trying to get you into bed with Keil. Well, yeah, I am. The sooner, the better. Because if you don't get marked and mated before the weekend, Keil's wolf is going to be so agitated that I'm afraid for the outcome of the challenge."

TJ swung his gaze back to meet hers. "I'm afraid for you too, because it could be dangerous to be around the pack. Since you and Keil kissed and snuggled last night, your wolf has started to rise to the surface, and you're giving off sex pheromones like crazy. All of the unmated males are going to be real interested. I don't think Keil's aware of it because he's attracted to you already. I feel it, but I know you're his and I'm making myself ignore it."

Robyn nodded her understanding and reached to brush TJ's cheek in thanks with a quick touch. His eyes closed for a second, then he coughed.

"Um, Robyn? You need to know, wolves are into touchy-feely stuff, and as much as I like you to touch me, you'd better not do that again until after you and Keil get hitched. 'Cause right now I don't think he could stand to scent you on anyone, and I'm kinda fond of my balls staying attached to my body."

He handed back the water bottle and motioned for her to take the lead up the hill.

They climbed, using the long shallow switchbacks Keil had set to make the ascent easier. Robyn glanced over her shoulder to see TJ following behind, slow and steady, his skis skittering off to the side every few steps. He was terribly uncoordinated on two feet.

By the time they reached the top of the pass, Robyn was sweating nicely and feeling a warm glow of satisfaction from the exertion. Keil had pulled out a small cook stove and fired it up to heat water for a drink.

"You're a good skier, Robyn. Kept the pace nicely." Keil's compliment warmed her as she sat facing him, able to look over the mountains that ranged downward to the Pacific Ocean and still see his face. She breathed a relaxed sigh as she let her gaze wander over the sunlit peaks. A squeeze on her knee brought her attention back to Keil.

"Are you hungry?"

She nodded and pulled her pack closer to dig out the food she'd brought. She passed him a couple of her homemade granola bars and watched with pleasure the expression on his face as he bit into them.

"These are delicious. Did you buy them in Whitehorse?"

She shook her head *no* and nodded *yes* while pointing to herself.

"You didn't buy them, but you got them. Did you make them?"

She nodded.

The admiration in Keil's eye's increased. "Hmmmm. She cooks too." He leaned forward slowly and planted a gentle kiss on her lips. They stared at each other for a minute, desire rising between them like a tangible cloud before the boiling water brought Keil back to earth.

"You guys are too fast." TJ's red face as he dropped beside Keil made Robyn laugh. "Oh sure, laugh it up at the slowpoke. I'll have you know that once you can shift to wolf, I'll be able to beat your butt in a race anytime. Right, Keil?"

Keil handed Robyn a cup of hot sweet tea. "Other than suggesting you not even think about Robyn's butt ever again, I will agree that you are very fast as a wolf. Robyn, I know this has been an information overload with everything we've thrown at you—"

Robyn waved her hand to cut him off. She deliberately

turned her back on him and pointed over the mountains, over the whole panorama until she faced them.

"She's right, Keil. Shut up for a minute and enjoy the view."

"I know but—"

"But nothing. It's too hard to talk right now. Relax. Or don't you know how? You need to lighten up a little, bro. It's not all pack politics, life-and-death situations, Captain Kirk, I mean Keil, to the rescue."

When TJ finished speaking, Robyn glanced at Keil and nodded. She held her hand to him and he rose to join her. She pulled off her glove to trace her fingers down his cheek before twisting around and settling her back against him as she admired the view.

He was very serious, Robyn realized. He couldn't be much older than she was, and he was planning on taking on the leadership of a large group of, well, if she guessed right, rather headstrong individuals.

She could help him learn to relax. She stifled a giggle.

Keil's strong arms supported her, coming around her torso and pulling her tight into his rock-solid frame. Too bad winter clothing made everything extra bulky, but she could still appreciate the feel of his firm body.

She turned and slipped her hands behind his neck. As their lips brushed together, she tightened her hold and lifted her feet off the ground to let her full body weight drag at him.

The surprise move worked and they fell to the snow. Robyn tried to slip away as they hit the ground but he held her as he rolled to end up lying on top of her, pinning her in place.

"That was sneaky, Robyn." Keil stared at her, shifting his hips to let her know she was trapped. "I think you should pay a forfeit for that little trick." He lowered his head and nuzzled against her neck, and Robyn felt him taking deep breaths. His tongue shot along her bare skin, and she shivered as a wave of desire scurried through her body, over her breasts and settled in her womb like a ticking time bomb.

Man, oh man, this guy was potent.

With a final kiss to her neck Keil rose from her body and pulled her to her feet.

"It's getting late and if we want to get back to the cabin in daylight, we'd better ski. Stay away from the right side on the descent, the snow seems unstable." Robyn nodded, swallowing hard from the extra moisture in her mouth. Keil traced a finger over her lips and winked at her. "I'll claim my forfeit back at the cabin."

The three of them packed up their things, and this time Robyn led the way, skiing down the side of the mountain using telemark turns. She stopped a quarter of the way down and waited for the others to catch up. Keil stopped beside her, TJ farther to the side.

"Nice turns, Robyn." Keil said. "Let me go first, I want to watch you from below this time." He set off, making the lunging motions that cause cross-country skis to turn in the deep snow of the mountainside.

Robyn admired his skill as well. The people that she and Tad skied with in the mountains were all experts and Keil would fit in just fine. She caught up with him and they both turned to watch TJ do his descent.

His bright red jacket looked good on him and that was the most positive thing she could say about his technique. TJ didn't ski, he threw his legs about in a mad scramble like he was wearing rollerblades. Ski poles rotated in the air, snow flew everywhere. Robyn bit her lip to keep from laughing.

Then her breath caught in her throat. She saw the snow slab drop and a large crack appear on the hillside above where

TJ headed, too far into the dangerous side and completely out of control.

Robyn stared in horror as the side of the mountain behind TJ slid away in an avalanche, pulling his windmilling figure down the slope to the right of them. The ground underfoot shook for a moment but the snow pack where they stood was solid enough. Frantically she looked back and forth over the settling powder and clouds of fine snow to try to see any sign of TJ.

Nothing but the disturbed surface of the mountainside greeted their eyes.

Chapter Six

His stomach dropped as the avalanche raced past them. By the time the rumble faded, Keil had his transmitter out and switched to "seek" mode. They didn't have much time to uncover TJ, but they did have longer than finding a human.

As long as TJ was conscious.

Keil turned to Robyn. She already had her transmitter in her hand. She was pale and her eyes seemed large enough to overwhelm her face, but she was going through each step methodically. Carefully.

He grabbed Robyn's face in his hands, making sure she watched him.

"You know how to use your monitor?"

Robyn nodded.

"Since you can't hear me if I shout, I want you to look at me every five paces, to be sure you're aware of any warning I give. Understand?"

Robyn nodded again even as she shuffled away from him. She pointed up the mountain.

"Yes, you go up. If I signal 'clear' like this"—Keil slapped his fists together and pointed away with one hand—"I expect you to ski away as fast as you can. Understand?"

Her face grew grim and tight.

"I mean it. If you get caught in another avalanche, I won't be able to save you both. Remember, TJ's a werewolf. He's stronger than a human. He's going to be all right. Let's go."

The two of them skied quickly to the edge of the avalanche field and began a back-and-forth search motion to triangulate TJ's position. Keil moved cautiously, his attention split between rescuing TJ and the need to keep Robyn safe. Letting his mate move away from him into the potential danger of another slide physically hurt.

His senses were on high alert. The sun reflecting off the snow seemed blindingly bright. The squeak of their skis on the rough snow surface became reassuring in its consistency. A few steps, a pause to check the monitor, a glance around the mountain. A flick of the eyes to see Robyn, then repeat the series.

The blinking light on his receiver grew stronger and he turned to follow its direction. The next time Robyn looked his way, he raised an arm and pointed.

Robyn double-checked her monitor and raised her arm, pointing downhill in a path that bisected across his angle.

They were narrowing the gap.

It was painfully slow work when every nerve in his body screamed for them to hurry before TJ's air ran out. Keil took a moment to call out. "TJ!" He yelled in the direction he hoped they'd find TJ, but there was no response.

A trickle of sound reached his ears.

A low rumble in the distance.

He lifted his gaze to examine the mountains around them, fearful of what he'd see.

The peak to their left released a cornice of snow, the slide shifting a cloud of powder into the air. Quickly Keil estimated the angle of the slide, whether it would reach them, set off another slide on top of them.

The slope of the mountain curved away and Keil breathed a sigh of relief as the loose snow slipped behind a distant ridge out of sight and out of range of danger. He looked up to see Robyn watching intently for his signal. Escape or continue?

He pointed forward and Robyn nodded, trusting his judgment to continue her sweeping movements.

Her harsh shout a few moments later made his heart pound. He looked up to see her turning her ski pole into a depth probe. She pushed it through the snow to search for an air pocket or a buried body. Keil struggled up to her level, whipped off his shovel and prepared to dig.

"TJ, can you hear us?" Keil roared.

A welcomed howl rose to his ears. Keil threw up a prayer of thanks as he shoveled, Robyn working at his side. They dug into the hillside from the bottom to take advantage of the slope, trusting there would be less digging at that level. Soon Keil held out a hand to caution Robyn and get her attention.

"I don't want to strike him. Let me dig, you watch for additional slides."

Keil increased his speed, hearing TJ's howl grow clearer.

"Stay back from the shovel if you've got the room," Keil shouted as he swung at a furious pace. It was only a few more shovelfuls before he broke into the human-sized air pocket that contained the smaller wolf-sized body that was TJ. Keil watched as his brother scrambled out of the hole and, in his wolf body, circled around their legs in thanks.

✧

TJ sat in front of the fire in the cabin sipping a steaming

cup of hot chocolate. He'd run beside them all the way to the cabin as a wolf, his gear buried somewhere back on the hill.

"I still don't get it. What part of 'stay away from the right, the snow is unstable' did you not understand?" Keil complained, dropping an extra blanket around TJ's shoulders.

"Enough, I'm sorry. I got my lefts and rights mixed up. No harm done since Robyn made me put on the tracer. You found me, I'm fine."

"TJ, that's the third set of skis you've lost this year!"

The sound of logs crashing to the floor made both of them look up at Robyn's stunned expression. She lifted a trembling hand to show three raised fingers, a questioning expression on her face.

"Yeah," Keil said, "this is the third time Mr. Disaster has been in action this winter. His record is six times in a single season. I'm thinking of having a tracer permanently implanted—"

"Umm, Keil, why is Robyn glaring at me like that?"

Keil glanced up and he could have sworn he saw steam pouring out Robyn's ears.

Just before she leapt across the room, grabbed TJ by the throat and shook him.

Hard.

"Whoa, there, Robyn." Reaching around her, he gently grasped her forearms and loosened them from TJ's neck. Muttering soothing words even though he knew she couldn't hear, he settled her under his chin as her body continued to shake. "My guess is she's a little shocked that we had to rescue you in the first place, TJ, and learning this is a typical experience in the bush with you might be more than she needed on top of everything else today."

TJ had the grace to look embarrassed. He shuffled over and

squatted to peer up at Robyn where she hid in Keil's arms. "I'm sorry I scared you. I don't think sometimes. I won't do it again."

"Ha!" Keil snorted. "Don't make promises you can't keep, little brother. The sauna should be hot by now. Go get warmed up all the way. Robyn and I need to talk."

TJ shot another concerned glance at Robyn before gathering his clothes and heading out the door.

Keil settled down on the chair by the fire, still holding Robyn in his embrace as they sat quietly together. Having her in his arms felt wonderful. She was small enough to treasure yet strong enough to react in a quick and fearless manner when faced with the emergency on the mountainside. She was going to be a fabulous mate for him.

She smelt wonderful too. He took in a deep breath and fought down the urge to throw her on the sleeping platform and rip off her clothes.

Her fingers slipped up and traced the edge of his jaw, and Keil shut his eyes to enjoy the sensations tingling through his blood. She wiggled and he looked down to see she was shaking silently, tears trickling from her eyes.

"Hey, it's okay." He tilted her head back to reassure her and stopped at the expression on her face.

Sheer delight.

"What's up, little bird?"

Robyn wiped at her eyes and crawled off his lap, stopping only to plant a kiss on his cheek. She returned to his side with her notepad, dragging up another chair so they could face each other but both still enjoy the fire's warmth.

It may seem insane but I'm so happy right now, Robyn wrote.

"Happy? Having to rescue my brother makes you happy? Leaving him buried for once would make me ecstatic."

A snort of laughter from Robyn made Keil smile.

"Tell me, how can having your whole world turned upside down like we've done to you today make you happy?"

Robyn stared at him for a minute and bent her head to write. She handed him the note pad while she signaled like she was drinking from a glass.

Keil turned to read her message as she went to the water bucket.

All my life I've been different. But it's been bad different. It's hard to share with new people. My only friends my brother and old family friends.

But you accept me right away. You trust me right away.

Your brother is an idiot right away! You're real with me.

All that makes me very happy.

Keil lifted his head to see Robyn watching him with her big brown eyes, a soft smile on her lips.

"You have been different, but it's not because you're deaf. It's because you were supposed to be a wolf. You were supposed to be around your pack who would love you and support you. That's what's been missing." He took the glass she held out to him and placed it to the side with care before pulling her back into his arms.

"I won't rush you, and you probably still have a ton of questions but, Robyn, you need to know that I'll do anything for you. The connection between us is growing stronger, and I'm glad that I've found you." He leaned down and kissed her.

Soft. Gentle. A kiss of exquisite tenderness. He put his heart into the motion, trying to tell her without words that she didn't have to worry about him and that all the concerns of the day would work out fine in the end.

"How can I feel this connected with someone I just met?"

Keil froze.

He'd heard her voice in his mind.

Pulling back from her he stared into her eyes. He thought it would happen, but not already. They weren't even mates yet. She hadn't had her wolf triggered.

It was impossible.

"How did you do that?" Keil asked.

Her face grew puzzled and Keil tried to paste on a smile. It must have not worked because Robyn pulled away.

"Wait, try something for me. Tell me your favorite colour."

After giving him the "are you insane" look she did oh-so-well, she reached for the notepad.

"No writing. Try and tell me in my head."

Robyn stared at him. *"He's doing the crazynut thing again. I don't have a favorite colour to tell him."*

"Everyone has a favorite colour, Robyn."

All the colour drained from her face. *"Did you hear me?"*

Keil stroked her cheek and attempted to speak to her mind. *"Yup, it goes well with the 'crazynut thing' that I do."*

Robyn scrambled backward off his lap, ending up in a pile on the floor.

"Holy shit! You can hear me. I can hear you! How is this possible, Keil?" She pulled herself up to her knees and hugged his legs tightly. Then she dragged herself upright until they were eye-to-eye. *"Say something else to me."*

"You're the most beautiful thing I've ever seen."

She blew a raspberry at him. *"Say something intelligent."*

Instead he dove at her mouth, trailing kisses over her lips and flowing down the edge of her neck to bury his face in the V of her shoulder. *"You're beautiful and you smell like a spring meadow. Your skin feels fresh and clean like the wind blowing over the glacier. You taste like a fresh-caught fish with a good glass of wine."*

"You poet, you. You're making me hungry."

Keil lifted his head and stared into her eyes. *"You make me hungry too, and I'm planning on doing something about it. I wanted to wait but..."*

Her fingers laced into the hair at the back of his neck. *"This is crazy. My body feels like I'm on fire. How can I hear you? You said this morning that mates could sometimes speak like this but we're not mates. I mean, doesn't that require us to have sex first?"*

"It usually does, Robyn. The only thing I can think of is the adrenaline rush from the avalanche triggered you and started to link us. You're an exceptionally strong wolf, and so am I. Not that I'm bragging or anything."

Robyn blinked at him and he grinned back as he stood, lifted her and took a step toward the sleeping platform. He stopped and checked around the room. Shaking his head he turned back, his need for her growing stronger.

"Damn, I want you. But not here. Get your things together."

"We're going to have sex? Now?"

She was thinking so hard Keil could hear the echo of her concern bounce off the mountainside. *"Now. And if that means we not only trigger your wolf, we get you pregnant at the same time, we'll hold a double celebration. You're my mate, Robyn. That means lots of great sex and a family to boot. Whenever it happens, sooner or later. You have any trouble with that?"*

Her shy glance up into his face almost undid him.

Chapter Seven

Robyn shifted uncomfortably on the bench in the annex outside the sauna. Keil had gone back into the cabin with TJ and left her with the directions to relax and wait for him while he grabbed a few things. She added a couple extra logs into the stove, topped up the snow in the buckets and sat to wait.

It was damn uncomfortable to be sitting there knowing any moment a werewolf was going to walk in the door and have sex with her.

Arghhhh. Even the thought made her twitch. What the hell was she doing? This was crazy. It was beyond crazy.

The door opened and Robyn jumped. Sexual heat flowed off Keil's body and reached to caress her skin.

Okay. She remembered why she was going to do this. Every inch of her was on fire and she was being drawn toward the tall, hard male as if she had ropes that twined about her limbs, trapping her. Keil dropped a blanket on the bench beside her. He glanced at her before lifting her chin with his hand.

"Hey, it's okay. Let's take this slowly."

Robyn dropped her eyes, blushing furiously. *"I'm scared."*

"Scared of me?"

"Kind of."

His gentle hand traced over her ear and nestled in the hair

at the back of her neck. *"I don't want to scare you, little bird. I want to love you."*

She lifted her eyes to his. *"I don't know what to do. I mean, I* know *what to do but I've never..."*

Keil waggled his eyebrows and his eyes brightened. "I know you've never. I'm glad you've never. It's good that you've never. Now I don't have to go track down your old lovers to kill them."

"Possessive much?"

"You have no idea. Yet." Keil leaned closer to brush his lips over hers. *"Wait until you are fully wolf. I bet you're going to be just as possessive about me. Wolves mate for life, and we don't like to share."*

Robyn shifted again on the hard bench. How could she want this much and still feel afraid to take the next step? She closed her eyes and took a deep breath, trying to build up her courage.

A gentle touch pulled her to her feet. *"You're thinking too hard. Let's go slow. You must be sweaty from our ski and digging up TJ. Let me help wash you up."*

Keil's hands drifted over her shoulders, pulling her up against his body for a brief caress as he reached behind her body to grasp the bottom of her long-sleeved T-shirt. With a slow fluid motion, he lifted it off her, then dropped it on the bench behind them.

As his eyes traced over her torso, Robyn fought the urge to cover her chest with her hands. Ugh. She had to decide to be seduced in a mountain cabin wearing her plainest and sturdiest underwear. Luckily Keil's face didn't seem to express any displeasure with what he saw.

And neither could Robyn complain. Keil removed his own shirt with one swift yank and stood inches away from her, his rock-solid abs tempting her fingers.

"Damn. Just...damn. Is what they mean by washboard abs? Can I do some laundry?"

Keil smiled and reached for her. Removing the tight sports bra didn't go as smoothly. In the middle of pulling it off, Keil's hand got stuck in the twist of the Y back and Robyn froze with her arms pulled over head, bra wrapping her tight with Keil's forearm. Heat rose to her face.

"Hell of a thing to happen, but don't worry. This gives us some very interesting possibilities." Keil lowered his head to press a kiss on her neck, fluttering soft kisses down over the tops of her exposed breasts, sending chills shooting through her even as he supported and stretched her arms above them.

His touch was gentle but the restrained power was there, under the surface. His tongue stroked over her skin toward her cleavage then his teeth nibbled back up the line of heat he'd created all the way to her lips. His hand was loose from her bra and she lowered her arms slowly, his hot gaze never leaving her body.

"Take off the rest and I'll get the shower ready." He spun around quickly, leaving Robyn wondering what she'd done wrong.

"Keil?"

His strong arms poured the heated water into the holding tank over the top of the shower. *"I need to cool off a bit. You're very beautiful and because you're my mate, I really, really want you. I'm trying to keep things slow here."*

After prepping the water, he placed her into the shower, turning her body until she was wet from head to toe. With a flick of the wrist, he stopped the water and picked up the washcloth and soap. Starting at the back of her neck, he rubbed small circles over her skin, covering her shoulder blades, slipping over her spine until his hands cupped both cheeks of her ass.

Robyn dropped her forehead against the side of the shower stall and closed her mind to everything but the wonderful sensations racing over her skin at his touch. The heat from the sauna warmed the side room they were in to the point that she was comfortable even as droplets continued to cling to her skin. His mouth fastened on her neck, lapping at stray pebbles of water pooled there. Her womb clenched, releasing moisture as every stroke of his tongue sent thrills through her body to increase the desire mounting deep inside.

His touch dropped lower as Keil squatted behind her, his hands caressing down one leg. The small circular motions were driving her crazy as he teased, moving closer to the core of her heat and retreating without satisfying.

"Turn around, beautiful."

Keil's voice in her mind was deep and dark. It sounded like rich chocolate and Robyn was so into chocolate.

His voice made the tingles race.

Robyn pivoted to face Keil as he continued to kneel in front of the shower stall. She gazed down at him and was shocked by the powerful look of need reflected up at her. He drew a shaky breath, dipped his washcloth into the warm water he had by his side and the torment began again.

Only now Robyn could watch him as well as feel his touch. He dropped his gaze to her body as he washed her feet carefully before he moved up her legs. She reached out a hand to caress over his head, enjoying the erotic feel of his hair under her fingers. She bent over and loosened his ponytail holder, combing out the braid to watch the dark strands pour over his shoulders in a fountain of dark silk.

His attention had reached the level of her pussy and she drew in a sharp breath as he licked his lips and shot her a glance hot enough to make her melt. The cloth dipped and this time Keil lifted it still dripping to softly touch her folds. The warm water ran over her skin, slipping into the crevices hidden from his eyes only to continue the journey down her legs in slow rivulets.

Keil dropped the cloth to the side and used both hands to part her to his gaze. Robyn shivered at the intimate touch and closed her eyes only to have them shoot open at the feel of his tongue darting against the small nub he had exposed.

"Ohhh."

Keil's mouth lowered on her, his tongue gentle as it slipped up and down the sides of her labia, each pass including a circle around the tip of her clitoris.

While one hand held her open, the fingers of the other dipped lower, and Robyn felt him explore her pussy, tracing circles in the moisture he found there.

"Oh, babe, you are extremely beautiful. You may have never made love before, but your body knows what to do. Feel how wet you are, Robyn? That's your body getting you ready for me. You're wet and hot and..." his tongue dipped lower to thrust up into her depths, *"...and oh-so-tasty."*

Robyn was sure she was going to collapse; she shook as the assault on her pussy continued. Keil raised one of her legs and placed it over his shoulder, opening her more to his touch. He reached up and pressed back on her torso until she leaned on the shower wall, then his hands came and supported her hips.

With that single motion she was held in his grasp, completely at his mercy as his mouth increased its tempo, licking and caressing every inch of her pussy, his hot breath bathing her limbs. The tension inside her was rising, closer and closer to exploding when one hand dropped back down and he slipped a finger into her passage and stroked in and out.

"Robyn, does it feel good? I want you to enjoy this."

She tried to engage her brain enough to speak to him, but

it was impossible. She was a puddle of warm goo, and if he wasn't careful, she was going to slip down the drain. The tingles had been replaced by electrical zaps that could power a small village, and she was panting hard enough she was in danger of hyperventilating.

A second finger joined the first and the feeling of fullness countered with the exquisite torture on her clit sent her over a cliff with an explosion that knocked her off her remaining leg. Supported only by Keil's hands and the wall behind her Robyn's body squeezed hard around his fingers, moisture drenching him as his tongue continued to lap at her.

"Hmmm, you don't need to talk. I know you liked that. You are delicious." He kissed a trail up to her bellybutton, then stood her on her feet. His tender touch supported her until she stopped swaying. He flicked on the tap and the warm water of the shower slid over her skin. Keil's hands brushed soft and gentle over her back, rinsing away the soap he'd used earlier. As the water stopped Robyn opened up her eyes to stare directly into his face.

Heat and deep need shone back at her. Wrapping his arms around her, Keil lifted her and walked into the sauna, leaving the door open behind them. He sat on the widest bench and arranged her on his lap facing him.

Kisses like a ten-car pile-up were followed by his hands soft and gentle over her breasts. Robyn let her head fall back as Keil palmed one breast and lowered his mouth to the other, lapping and suckling at the rosy tip until it hardened to a peak. He switched his attention to the other side, each tug of his mouth sending another streak of desire from her nipple to her core, tension building as her desire for Keil grew stronger.

He smelt good. He felt even better.

Robyn let her fingers wander over his shoulders and down his torso as he made love to her breasts. Slipping her fingers through his hair she felt the connection between them growing tighter, more concentrated. Tendrils of emotion, not only desire but affection and friendship, wrapped around her.

More than sex, they were definitely making love.

Robyn lifted her head to stare at Keil. He sat back and leaned against the wall. His eyes were full of raw emotion.

"Did you feel that? That was... Wow."

"I felt it. Wow is right. Robyn, touch me."

He took her hand and led it down to his cock where it stood rigid between their bodies. He was so hard the swollen head tapped his belly, a drop of moisture clinging to the small slit. As Robyn's fingers softly stroked him, velvet over steel, Keil's eyes closed and a shiver ran through his body.

Robyn swallowed hard. She used both hands to explore, trying not to freak out at how big it seemed. *"Umm, Keil? I think I'm afraid again. No way will this thing fit in me. Ugh. I've read that in stories before and it sounded stupid, but seriously, you are hung like a damn horse."*

Keil's laughter shook his body. *"And in all the stories you've read, does the 'thing' fit?"*

"Yes, but—"

"No butts, not today." Keil's strong hands slapped gently on her ass cheeks. *"We'll save that for another time."*

"Now you're really scaring me!"

Keil lay on the bench and made Robyn straddle his body, his cock pressed hard along the cheeks of her ass. His hands continued to smooth over her back, her breasts, her belly. Each stroke raised Robyn's temperature as the tremors grasped her.

His fingers touched her clit, making small circles along the wet lips of her pussy until he pushed her over the edge into another orgasm.

When her breath was halfway back to normal, Keil lifted her hips up and supported her over the tip of his cock. She took her weight onto her knees and he used one hand to rub the wet head of his shaft against her pussy lips again and again.

"Ride me. Go as slow as you want."

She reached down and joined her hand to his as he directed his cock into the warm depths. Robyn watched Keil's face. Tenderness reflected in his eyes, dark need and desire.

She pressed down, freezing as the mushroomed head of his shaft stretched her wide. The sides of her passage were wet but she felt every bump and vein as his heat stroked her.

"Oh lordy, that feels good."

"Little bit more, babe."

Each tiny movement of her hips fed the fire building in her belly until the pressure shot to pain and she hesitated.

"Keil?"

"Lean forward, and let me have those beautiful lips for a minute."

His mouth met hers and she tangled their tongues together, letting Keil take control of her hips as he continued to rub against her. His tongue licked down the corner of her mouth to lap at her neck and her brain shut down. He suckled at her skin then put his teeth on her.

One solid thrust with his hips drove him through her barrier to rest balls deep inside her pussy. Simultaneously he bit down on her neck and the joint pleasure/pain of the two piercings flashed through Robyn's body, her inner walls clutched at his cock, her hands tangled in his hair.

"Sweet mercy, what have you done to me?"

He pulled her torso against his body and held her tight, waiting as she adjusted to his girth stretching her. The feel of his hard body under her hands, the beating of his heart mixed with the pleasure still tingling through her washed away the remnants of pain.

Slowly he began to move her, pulling her hips high to let the tip of his cock cling to her entrance, then slipping her all the way down, angling his thrusts to go as deep as possible.

Robyn pushed her body upright so she could watch, one hand pressed to Keil's chest, one hand dropping to feel where they connected to each other. The intimacy of touching his cock, having it brush along her fingers as it slipped into her body made her head spin with delight. Keil smiled up at her and added his hand to hers, linking fingertips, rubbing against her clit with each drive of his hips.

She pressed down in tempo with his thrusts, needing him to go faster, go deeper. The air from the sauna around them seemed to cool as their bodies warmed to boiling, passion driving higher and higher until Robyn climaxed once more, her sheath milking his cock as Keil exploded, the warmth of his seed bathing her with fire deep inside. He clung to her hips, holding her tight until the tremors subsided.

Limbs tangled, Robyn's head resting on his chest, Keil felt the tendrils of connection finish and settle into his soul.

His mate.

He stroked one hand over her hair, brushing the strands back off her face to stare at her soft skin. Her bright eyes shone up at him with a touch of bewilderment and a whole lot of satisfaction. Robyn's full lips were wet from where she'd licked them and Keil felt himself hardening at the thought of leaning down to nuzzle at her mouth.

"How are you, little bird?"

"That was...well actually, that was amazing. If I'd known it

was going to be this much fun I'd have tried it sooner. Keil? Are you growling at me?"

Keil pulled back the anger he'd had flash through him at the thought of anyone touching Robyn.

"Sorry, love, under control now. How about we do it again if you enjoyed it that much? Or try a few other things?"

"Not the butt, wolfman, you're not going there. What should we do about TJ? He's sitting in the cabin all alone."

Keil lifted her and carried her back to the shower, gently rinsing the signs of their lovemaking off her limbs, caressing softly over her pussy and stirring her fires again.

"Actually, TJ isn't in the cabin anymore. I told him to go home. He may not be able to ski by himself, but since the silly boy lost all his equipment in the accident, he'll have to run home as a wolf anyway. We'll meet him in Haines Junction at the condo the pack owns. The cabin is all ours. Welcome to our honeymoon suite."

Robyn touched his cheek and pulled him into the shower stall with her. She picked up the cloth to wash his chest, rubbing the trail of dark brown hair that led down to more interesting territory.

"That's the best news I've heard in a while. Keil?"

Keil had closed his eyes as Robyn's fingers traced over his shaft, one hand stopping to cup his balls, the other slipping from side to side over the velvety soft skin on the head.

"Yes, Robyn?"

"It fit. It fit just fine."

Chapter Eight

Keil managed to keep one hand tucked around Robyn even as he finished scooping up the rest of the noodles from the dinner pot. He never seemed to be far away. He touched her constantly. Over the past three days, they had made love in the sauna, in the cabin, even enjoyed a quick romp on the porch under the moonlight. One night Keil had eaten a piece of cheesecake off her belly then proceeded to lick every inch of her thoroughly before taking her quivering body to the shower house to continue.

When they weren't making love they skied, built a snow fort and talked for hours about everything.

Robyn couldn't decide whether she liked the talking or the loving better. Being with Keil was amazing. There were definitely benefits to this mate thing.

"It's only Tuesday but I think we should ski out tomorrow like TJ and I had planned. There's a lot we need to do before Saturday."

Robyn nodded hesitantly.

"What, little bird?"

She pressed her lips against his cheek. *"I don't want to go home yet. This is the shortest honeymoon on record."*

"Oh, the honeymoon isn't over, sweetie. We'll have to delay the rest until after..." Keil broke off, his body tensing up next to

hers.

Robyn stood to clear away the dishes, fighting to keep tears from forming in her eyes. The pack challenge. She understood from their talks that it had to happen.

But she wasn't ready to share him yet. With anyone.

Keil swung her around to face him.

"This is not how I would have chosen to make you my mate, forcing changes on you this quickly. But we needed each other. I needed you. I won't apologize for taking advantage of finding you and loving you.

"You're going to have your first full moon as a wolf on Saturday, and the challenge isn't until Sunday. Come back to Haines with me and I will introduce you to the pack members who support me. I will win the challenge, Robyn. Especially now that I have you. Trust me."

"I do trust you, but I can't go to Haines. I'm supposed to phone my brother today, he's to meet me on Saturday at the trailhead. I have to talk to him if there's any changes and this is going to be tough to explain. Oh, hell."

Keil looked puzzled for a minute. "You said you had a satellite phone. How were you planning on using it? You can't hear."

"Text message."

"On a sat phone?"

"Ain't technology great?"

"I'd hate to know what that costs per message. Can I talk to your brother for you?"

Robyn considered. Tad was the kind to worry but he also knew when to back down. She thought Keil would be able to talk it out with her brother. It might, however, take a while.

"Only if you plan on paying the charges."

"What are you, cheap?"

"Like borscht."

Keil pulled her in for a kiss, the kind that made her toes curl and her heartbeat increase. Just as it was getting interesting, he broke it off. *"Damn, you get tastier and tastier. I'd better make that call before I get too distracted. What's the number?"*

Robyn pulled out the phone and handed him one of Tad's business cards that she kept with it. Keil choked for a second before flashing a big grin. Robyn paused as she sat at the table. What was Keil up to now? The expression in his eyes was way too mischievous.

Keil linked the call through and sat back to talk, making sure she could see his lips.

"Hi, Tad, this is Keil Lynus. How are you, man?" Keil winked at her and a warning signal went off in her brain. Something stunk. "No, TJ doesn't need any rescuing, we already dug him out... I know, he's a total pain in the butt. I do need something... She's fine. In fact Robyn and I are mates and I was—"

Robyn stared at Keil in shock. How could he blurt it out like that to Tad? Her brother must be freaking. She slapped at Keil's shoulder, trying to take the phone away from him.

"Hang on, Tad, she's getting a little frisky right now. I think she's worried you're having a fit or something over there. Want to talk to her?"

With a violent yank Robyn pulled the phone away from Keil to check the screen. Maybe he hadn't phoned anyone at all and it was a joke. But there was a return message on the screen.

Congratz, sis, Keil is awesome. I'm happy for u

Robyn's jaw dropped to the floor. She typed in quickly. *U know Keil? U know what he is?*

Ya. Wolf. u work fast sis

U are sooooo dead next time I c u Tad

luv U 2 Robyn

Jerk

Keil pulled the phone away, said “hi” and paused to listen for a minute.

“Well, thanks. It was a surprise but she’s incredible, Tad. Hey, there is a little thing shaking down this weekend if you’d like to join us. Robyn’s first full moon will be on Saturday... Of course you can come! You’re family, even if you aren’t triggered yet... I know, Tad.” Keil rolled his eyes. “It’ll happen sometime, man. Gotta go. Robyn’s making me pay for this call... I can afford it, but why would I want to spend more time talking to you when I can be with my mate?”

Robyn fought to control her breathing as Keil hung up and packed away the phone. The smirk on his face was more than she could handle and she pounded on his arm.

“Hey, what’s this? I thought that went rather well. Tad will even be able to join us for the full moon. Great, hey?”

“You ass. You never told me you knew my brother. How does he know you and how come he knew you were a wolf and—”

Keil wrapped his arms around her and lifted her off her feet, as she continued to struggle against him. Robyn fumed. Keil had known Tad all along. Tad knew about werewolves and never once said anything to her about the fact she was one.

Shit. That was probably the “big secret” he’d kept trying tell her.

They were both dead.

Keil lowered her to the sleeping platform and covered her body with his own, stopping her from being able to wiggle away.

The thrill of his touch battled with the desire to kick his kneecaps off.

"Tell me what's up, Keil, or I'll be forced to hurt you."

"You'd never hurt me."

"Oh yeah? Ever eaten a granola bar with a laxative additive? I can arrange it for you."

Keil laughed and rolled to the side, running a hand over her body as he spoke. "I didn't realize the connection when you said you were a Maxwell. You told me you had a brother but you never told me his name."

Robyn opened her mouth to protest but then froze. *"Damn. Are you sure?"*

Keil nodded. "I would have recognized the name. I know Tad from my guiding business. He flies us on trips all the time. He told me he had a sister, but he never said she was deaf. He found out we were wolves on a trip when TJ did one of his not-so-amazing Houdini tricks while Tad was still around.

"Your brother is a half-breed wolf, still untriggered. We guessed it was your Grampa who gave him the genes. If you're wondering, yes, he knew you were a wolf." Robyn tensed under his hands. "Hey, think of it this way. He can't shift until he gets triggered, and you know that's complicated for a male half-breed. Telling you about werewolves wasn't going to work because he had no proof. He probably thought your mate would be someone from one of the Whitehorse packs."

Robyn dropped her head back on the bunk with a flash of insight. *"Is that why he's been introducing me to all these different 'clients' over the years? Were they all wolves?"*

"Maybe. He did mean well, remember that before you slit his throat, my vengeful hussy." Keil's hands slid possessively over her. *"Since it's our last night here I vote we take advantage of it. Dinner was great but I want my dessert."*

He opened her shirt and proceeded to bury his head in her breasts, rubbing back and forth over her torso like he was painting himself with her scent.

"You can't tell, but you smell absolutely amazing, Robyn. It's something to do with being recently triggered as well as being my mate, but your pheromones are off the chart right now." He licked a long slow line up from between her breasts until he reached her lips and proceeded to tease the corners of her mouth with gentle nips and kisses.

"TJ said it could be a problem with the pack. That all the guys would be attracted to me."

Keil pulled back and stared at her for a second. "He's right, I never thought about that. I mean, you're marked as mine, and your scent is clearly our scent, but as a full-blood until after your first full moon, you're sending off killer hormones."

He traced a finger down her body, circling the globes of her breasts as he considered. "I'll be careful who I introduce you to. Only mated couples and females until after the weekend. You're too beautiful. I'd be fighting everyone for you otherwise."

"You wolves seem to like fighting."

"It passes the time and keeps us warm. It's cold in Alaska."

Robyn grabbed his hand from where it teased her and pushed it farther down her body until his strong fingers cupped her mound. She pressed her hips upward gently, encouraging him to explore. *"It's cold up here in the Yukon too, but I know of lots of other ways to stay warm. Fireplaces, hot tubs..."*

"...saunas, beds. I'm looking forward to trying them all with you." Keil spread his fingers over her belly and finally lowered his head to her breast. His tongue flicked to moisten the tip of her nipple. Her body responded and a tight peak formed. Keil's contented smile warmed her heart. He didn't simply go through the motions. He seemed to enjoy touching her, making her feel

wonderful.

He blew a stream of cool air over her breast, sending a shot of pleasure down to her womb. Keil's mouth lowered and he suckled the erect tip into his mouth, tugging sharply until on the edge of pain. He followed with a gentle lap. A delicate nip with his teeth. The alternating tugs and soft caresses built up the pressure burning deep in her core. She reached her hands to massage over his shoulders, holding him close to her body.

Suddenly she needed more. She wanted to touch him, make him feel as good as he made her feel. He'd been such a tender lover over the past days, but he'd been controlling as well, never letting her take charge.

"Keil...oh damn that feels good. I want you to roll over. Please?"

She felt his chuckle against her breast. *"You going somewhere, little bird?"* His mouth continued to feast on her as he pulled her into his arms and flipped them over, finishing with her nestled on top of him.

He was still suckling.

Robyn tucked up her legs to straddle Keil's strong body, giving her some leverage. She slowly lifted her torso away from his caresses. The expression of loss on his face made her smile.

"It's okay, wolfman, I'm not going anywhere but down."

His puzzled expression faded as heat flared in Keil's eyes. Robyn winked and started the exploring she wanted to do.

His body was amazing, and all hers to enjoy. Taut chest muscles that flexed under her hands, nipples that tightened as she stroked her fingers over their tips. He seemed to enjoy her touch there as much as she had enjoyed his. She lowered her mouth to lick gently at the erect tip.

His body jerked. Yup, he liked it too. Robyn copied his earlier example and blew. Another body jerk followed.

"You're killing..."

She moved farther south, her tongue lapping the edges of the six-pack that had impressed her that first night together, the ridges sharp and defined as his muscles clenched with anticipation.

"Please..."

Robyn slid between Keil's thighs as she descended his body. She paused, resting on her elbows, to examine him in all his glory. His erect cock saluted her only inches away. The head had turned a rich purple shade, a bead of moisture shining on the slit. The edges of the mushroom-shaped top sloped sharply to the rigid shaft.

She slipped out the tip of her tongue. Soft, tentative in her touch.

"Holy..."

Robyn flicked a glance up to see Keil's dark eyes flashing at her. She liked that he was unable to complete full sentences. She liked the way his body responded to her touch. She must be doing something right.

Heat poured off him and the scent of raw sex in the air was driving her wild. She grinned, and maintaining eye contact, she sucked the head of his cock into her mouth.

His eyes rolled back in his head and his six-pack tightened further. If that was possible.

Robyn fell into a rhythm, a swirl of her tongue over the edge of the rim followed by an attempt to take as much of Keil into her mouth as possible. The first couple of times she gagged a little as the crown of his cock hit the back of her throat. The wetter her mouth got, the easier it was to slip him past her lips even as she felt him grow harder. Thicker.

Her excitement grew as well. Touching Keil, pleasuring him like this, turned her on big time, getting her all hot and bothered. She closed her eyes and hummed with delight.

"Damn it, that's enough. I'm not wasting this."

Keil's powerful arms lifted her away from his body and swung her around, finishing with his body pressed hard to her back. His cock nestled between her legs and Robyn instinctively threw out her arms to catch her body before it could hit the mattress.

"I was enjoying myself! I wanted to make you feel good."

"Babe, I feel great. But I don't want to come in your mouth tonight. I want your hot, tight body to squeeze me. I want to feel you milk me when you come. Tonight is for both of us. Now, open your legs wider."

Keil's hand smoothed over her hip and pressed her body lower to the mattress, exposing her more clearly to his gaze.

"Damn, you are beautiful. Everywhere. Like a flower opening up to me, dew glistening on the petals." He shifted his body away, letting his fingers dip into her passage. He drew some of her cream up, bringing moisture toward the tight rosebud hidden between her cheeks. She stiffened, trying to wiggle away from the exploring finger that circled, touched. Teased.

"Whoa, I'm not sure about that."

"Hush. I'm not going to do anything you won't like. Someday I'm going to take you in the ass, but not today. Today I'll show you something special. Trust me."

His hands were everywhere. Slipping over her breasts, tweaking her nipples to hard needy peaks before swirling over her belly and pressing intimately against her clit. A finger slid inside her, stroked a few times then withdrew, leaving her feeling empty. Then he started all over.

Robyn pressed her hips back, trying to make contact with his body. *"No more teasing. I need you. Please."*

Suddenly he was there, skin-to-skin with her, his hard, hot

cock against her core. Keil leaned forward and his mouth latched onto her shoulder. He sucked hard, his teeth pressing the skin. He covered the place where he'd marked her earlier, and as he sucked, a bolt of lightning flashed through her and set off an orgasm that she swore shook the cabin.

And the mountain. Possibly the entire territory, but she could be mistaken about that.

Then he surged into her in one smooth motion that set off another explosion that registered on the Richter scale.

Damn, he was good.

Keil set up a smooth pace that buried his entire length deep inside her on every thrust, his balls slamming into her. His hands held her hips firmly and he used them to pull her back even more forcibly onto him as his speed picked up.

"I've wanted you like this since the beginning, Robyn. You can't know how much it turns me on to see you in front of me, spread for my pleasure, your breasts swaying. You're so hot and wet and tight around me. Your ass is beautiful, smooth and inviting." He shifted one hand to run over the sensitive nerves of her anus, dipping a finger past the rim even as he continued to pump into her with his cock.

Robyn's body was on overload. She hadn't come down from the last climax and every nerve in her body tingled. Her breasts rubbed the sleeping bag every time Keil entered her. His shaft seemed to grow in size as Keil's finger pressed even farther into her ass to start a rhythm in time with the thrusts of his cock. The double penetration made her grow wetter than ever as all the sensations drew to another peak. The unending in and out strokes built heat where she thought there was nothing left to burn.

His free hand slipped around her body to touch her clit and she screamed, the wildfire ripping through her consuming every available inch of skin and tissue. Keil's body slammed into her one last time and she felt the flood of warmth from his release, felt the hard length within her jerk again and again as his hands locked them together.

It was hours later, she was sure of it, before she had enough energy to even draw a breath of air into her lungs. Her body tingled from top to bottom, although she had to admit that the bottom area tingled a bit more than anywhere else.

Keil's body reluctantly pulled away from her and she mourned the loss. She was resting on the platform trying to catch her breath, head down and butt up in the air, when a soft warm cloth slipped over her. Keil cleaned her up with such a gentle touch she wasn't even sure he was there the whole time.

He picked her up and held her close as he sat them in front of the fire. She slipped a hand over his jaw and smiled at him. His dark eyes stared down, the heat of passion still there, but something else as well. Something gentle and deep and forever.

Robyn laid her head against Keil's chest. She swore that she heard his heart beating.

For her.

Only for her.

Chapter Nine

The ski out with Keil was a hoot. He didn't take the straight route down the hills, instead veering off into the trees and making teleturns as often as possible.

Just like Robyn liked to do.

Usually it drove Tad crazy, but here was her mate doing the same insane thing. It felt great, and it was tons of fun to have someone to ski with who didn't freak out every time she left the main trail.

They made it down to the level of the second lake after an hour. The small hunter's cabin at the head of the lake was in disrepair but still a great place to stop for a hot drink and a short snack.

They were putting their gear back in their packs and getting ready for the ski across the lake when Robyn threw her arms around Keil and hugged him, hard. She was incredibly happy she could talk with Keil. Usually having to use sign language and read lips made the outward journey disjointed, but she could talk to him anytime.

She wondered how far away from each other they could be and still hear each other.

"What's up?"

"I love being with you. I love being able to speak into your mind and hear you in mine. I love skiing with you."

"I love skiing with you too, Robyn. Especially that little trick you have of squealing with delight before skiing over steep embankments."

Robyn hit him with a hastily formed snowball. *"I do not squeal."*

His gaze dropped over her body and heat rolled between them. *"You most certainly do squeal. And moan. And make all sorts of other delicious noises. Hell, I'm hard just thinking about it. Wanna fool around?"*

"Keil, it's twenty-five degrees out and we're in the middle of the forest. Cool your jets."

The leer he gave her as he reached down and adjusted himself promised some serious torture in the very near future.

"Do you realize how tough it is going to be to travel like this?"

"Put a ski on it. You'll be the fastest thing on three legs."

She danced away from him, laughing, and readied for the two-hour journey across the lake.

The snow pack was beautiful. Hard snow covered the surface with a heavy enough dusting of fresh powder to give their skis something to bite into. Once again Keil led the way, setting tracks for Robyn to follow. They continued to talk back and forth to each other easily about nothing in particular, avoiding discussing the pack, the challenge, everything controversial. Robyn enjoyed the rapid pace Keil set, and she was disappointed when he slowed down, glancing into the trees on their right.

"Hey, you getting tired or something?"

"Or something. Keep skiing but reduce your speed. Keep your eyes on my back. Understand?"

"No. We need to pick it up or we'll be in Haines in a week instead of a day."

"Are you watching my back?"

Robyn ran her eyes over the solid body in front of her. Her mouth watered at the thought he was all hers.

"Your backside, does that count? Yummy."

"Glad you think so. Don't freak out, but I think we're being shadowed. I count at least four wolves in the trees beside us. Are you still watching me?"

A shiver raced through Robyn. Something was very wrong or Keil would have simply stopped and faced the wolves. *"I'm watching you. What's up?"*

"Someone is trying to pull a fast one on us. If the other challenger to the Alpha position can take me out ahead of time, they can assume leadership. They must think you're TJ. People knew he was going to Granite with me."

"Yuck, what an insult. Have they never seen him ski? Wait, what do you mean 'take you out'? Hell, are they going to attack us?"

Keil continued to ski forward, Robyn narrowing the gap between them as his pace dropped. She slipped a couple of furtive glances toward the trees and spotted some of the wolves darting in and out of the distant tree line.

"Yeah, they're going to attack. Listen up. They don't know we're mates which means they don't know we can talk like this. That's to our advantage. If Jack were to do this right, he'd approach me alone and his seconds would stand back and watch. By sneaking up on us out here, I doubt Jack's planning on obeying any of the rules. If they think you're TJ, they're going to assume you'll fight like him." Keil paused. *"TJ's a tough wolf, Robyn. I'm guessing they will set two wolves on you."*

"Two wolves? That's not good odds, Keil, but if we stick together—"

"I want to, but we'd never survive that way. A four against

two means they can actually have three against one at times and even I can't fight that many at once without getting hurt. The thought is killing me, but I'm going to have to leave you for a bit. I'll attack the two that go after me, get at least one of them out of the picture, then rejoin you. I told you about wolf society and ranking. You're strong enough to hold them off."

They skied a bit farther as Robyn fought down her panic.

He was going to leave her and let two wolves attack her. No, that wasn't true. He was going to trust her to defend herself until he could come back and save them both.

That sounded better. Even if it still made her want to pee her pants.

"Right around this bend the wind usually blows the snow off the lake. The ice will be a better surface for you to stand on to defend yourself. We'll ski until we get there."

She didn't know if she wanted the ski to be over or to go on forever. Finally Keil lifted a hand as if signaling for a rest stop. He shifted his body to face the trees, casually turning her toward him.

Keil undid his clothes while hiding from the view of the trees behind Robyn's body. A dangerous gleam was in his eyes and an impression of power rolled off him. They might be in a tough place, but Keil was not going to be as easy a target as the others imagined.

"Protect your throat. If they're close enough to get at your throat, I want you to shove your arm into their mouth. They'll still be able to snap it and it'll hurt like hell, but your wolf can heal a busted arm. You can't regrow your throat."

Robyn gaped at him. *"Love you too, sweetheart. Man, you take your girl on the most romantic dates, don't you? Any other advice for me, Cujo?"*

Keil flashed a grin at her. "Just remember that kicking a

wolf in the nuts hurts as much as it does a human."

"Good to know, hon. So don't piss me off anymore, okay? What do you expect me to do, other than stand around looking like dinner?"

His answering smile reassured her more than it should have with wolves about to streak across the snow to try to kill her. "I expect you to use your ski poles, your big knife and your tough-as-nails attitude, and kick some butt for me. Ready?"

"You are sexy when you're all tough. I guess if they think I'm TJ I shouldn't lean over and plant a big one on your cheek right now, hmmm?"

Keil threw back his head and laughed. His arms reached out and while he kept his eyes on the tree line he kissed her thoroughly. *"What a wonderful idea. Now they're going to be worried about the sneak attack* and *freaking out watching us. Here they come. By the way, Robyn, I do love you."*

They drew a hands span apart. Robyn watched as Keil threw off his clothes and shifted to his wolf. His silver grey form raced toward the nearest of the wolves on the left. He flew across the snow and she cheered inside as she saw Keil's huge body slam into the smaller wolf and bowl him over.

Then she couldn't watch anymore as the wolves on the right closed in on her.

She turned and crouched, making sure that she had a firm grip on her knife. Her pack lay to the side and she made a mental note of its position to avoid tripping over it. Glancing back up toward the trees, she gasped.

"Damn it, you owe TJ an apology. They obviously think he's tougher than you realized. There are three wolves coming at me."

"I know. I've got three as well. Give me a second. Try and distract them."

Robyn grit her teeth together. Distract them? *"What, you*

want me to do a cancan dance or something?"

Fear and anger battled within Robyn. It was bad enough Keil was supposed to have to fight in the challenge this weekend. That at least was a time-honoured tradition and involved the values of fair play. This was nothing more than a sneak attack, cowardly and cheap.

She pulled the can of bear spray from her pocket where it had been stored since the start of the trip. One of the rules of the north was to never piss off anything you couldn't reason with.

Robyn was really pissed off.

She waited until the first wolf was in range, then lunged toward him as she held her breath and coated the beast with pepper spray. A four-second burst was enough and he howled in pain, scratching at his eyes with his paws as he rolled away from the fight, burying his face in the snow.

Dropping her knife and the bear spray, Robyn reached down to grab the straps of her pack. She swung around in a circle then let the pack fly into the next wolf, knocking him off his feet as she quickly retrieved her knife from the ground.

The remaining wolf was looking at her with his head tilted to the side like he was thinking really hard.

Like he was really confused about something.

A quick glance toward Keil showed her he'd taken one wolf to the ground. Keil's huge silver wolf body connected with another smaller black wolf and the two of them rolled in the snow, scratching at each other's torsos and necks with their claws.

"Steady, Robyn, I'm on my way. Watch the black wolf on you. He's Jack's brother and he's a mean one. The other wolf will try to distract you, but watch Dan."

Dan was still on the ground under the pack but he'd lifted

his head and was sniffing the air hard. He threw back his head and opened his mouth wide, and Robyn assumed that he was howling. Keil swore.

"Bloody hell. Run to me, NOW!"

Robyn turned, but Dan had regained his feet and lunged.

"I can't, he's attacking. What happened?"

"He's scented that you're my mate. He just told the others. Damn, I've got three on me again. Hold him off, babe, you can do it. He won't hurt you."

Robyn heard his anger even in her mind. Following Dan's cry the other wolf on her had left and he was attacking Keil, three on one. Robyn jumped aside as Dan nipped at her legs. Her backhand swing was too slow to do more than brush her knife against his fur before he withdrew a short way. His wolf eyes mocked her as he herded her away from where her mate continued to fight.

Keil was stronger than any one of the wolves around him, but his attackers teased, dancing out of reach of his claws and teeth.

"What are they doing?"

"They're trying to drag out the fight, tire me out before Jack even puts in an appearance."

Robyn pushed toward Keil, trying to narrow the gap between them, but she was frustrated time after time by Dan's lunges. She failed to see how close to the trees she'd been maneuvered.

Then she saw him.

Shit.

He was as big as Keil, black from tail to nose and he walked out of the woods straight toward her fearlessly.

"Keil, who's this asshole?"

Keil risked a quick peek and Robyn felt his anger flare. *"That's the chief asshole himself, Jack."*

She couldn't keep her eyes on both Dan and Jack at the same time, and all at once, something slammed into the back of her legs and she fell, hard, to the ice. Swinging with her arm she sliced with her knife and managed to hit meat this time. Her arm went numb and the blade flew from her fingers as her elbow was slammed to the ground by the weight of Jack's huge forepaw.

Her cry of distress reached Keil. *"Robyn, I'm coming. Hit him on the nose, kick him. Fight him."*

Robyn tried not to freak out. Jack's massive body lay on top of her, pinning her to the ground. He sniffed along her ear.

"I can't move. He's at my throat and he's got my arms pinned. He must weight five hundred pounds and oh my word, that is gross."

"I'm almost there. What did he do?"

"He licked my neck. Gack, he stinks."

Robyn strained to pull her legs up to be able to connect her feet with any part of Jack's anatomy. His muzzle continued to sniff along her throat, his tongue lapping occasionally as she struggled under him. He didn't seem to be trying to hurt her, but the sheer weight of his body forced the air from her lungs. Between that and the smell of his breath, she was growing light headed from a lack of oxygen.

Keil connected with the side of Jack's body and the two flew over her to roll toward the scraggy trees.

Teeth flashed. Jack was no longer holding back as he had with Robyn. The fury of the attack, the speed of the swinging claws, made her gasp in horror.

Fur literally flew.

But even after having fought the other wolves, Keil was

clearly stronger. His massive paws scrambled on the icy surface as Keil soon forced Jack down and over onto his back. Keil's teeth grasped Jack's throat and he placed a set of sharp claws against his opponent's belly.

He froze in position.

Waiting.

Robyn had crawled crablike away from their fight, mesmerized. She slowly became aware that while she waited nearby the other wolves still standing had surrounded her.

"Oh crap."

"They won't touch you. I've got their leader in a death grip. Physically he's been defeated and acknowledged my superiority."

The wolves circled her slowly, taking small lunges in her direction. Moving closer on each rotation.

"Are you sure that they know that? Because they're freaking me out here."

Robyn could see Keil's jaw moving, and she assumed he was talking to Jack. The black wolf threw back his head.

"Umm, Robyn? Slight problem. Remember TJ telling you about how being triggered made you smell kinda interesting right now?"

Robyn sidestepped another wolf that had moved closer in an attempt to brush up against her.

"Are you telling me these jerks have the hots for me?"

"Yup. We've got to convince them all that you're already taken. Including Jack, who just made a comment about how good you taste, by the way."

The four wolves circling Robyn turned and began to slink toward Keil. Tails low, teeth bared, it was clear they planned on attacking. He pressed his paw more firmly into Jack's belly, but there was no way he could defend himself without releasing his captive.

"Call them off me."

Robyn ran up to one of the nearer wolves and kicked him in the flank. He rolled away from her and continued on his route toward Keil. Desperately she tried to reach her mate's side, ignoring the pounding in her heart as she scrambled into the midst of six large wolves. The males avoided her, intent on their target.

"They're not paying attention, Keil. I have no weapon left."

"Just call them off. You've got a powerful voice and we're in the right here. It's our only chance. Do it now, Robyn!"

Throwing herself against Keil's side she cried out, "Stop. Leave him alone."

All the wolves froze except Keil.

He slowly removed his paw and backed away from Jack. Moments later Keil was back by her side after retrieving his clothes and her knife. He had an extremely pleased expression on his wolfy face. *"You are damn beautiful. And that voice—um, um good."*

Keil shifted and dressed as he spoke to her, finishing off by grabbing her and continuing the kiss he'd started before the attack.

"Keil, hello! Strange wolves loitering at our backs waiting to kill us, remember?"

With a final gentle nip to her bottom lip, Keil reluctantly pulled away.

"You are sexy when you use that Alpha voice. The puppies behind us? Take a look."

Robyn turned to see the wolves all lying belly down in the snow. When they saw her glance their way they dropped their muzzles to the ground and covered their eyes with their front paws.

Jack, bloody from Keil's attack, crawled forward on his belly until at their feet. His dark eyes darted back and forth between them, and then he slowly rolled to his back, exposing his throat.

Keil spoke aloud so the attackers could hear. "Shall we kill them?"

Robyn narrowed her eyes as she considered. *"Is the challenge still on for Sunday or did your competition just disqualify himself?"*

"Oh, Jack is very much out of any challenge for Alpha. In fact by the way they responded to your voice, I'd say you've shown we have complete power over them from now on."

Robyn dropped to her knees and pulled back sharply on Jack's ear, her knife close to his throat.

"Careful, babe. Think about it."

"Oh, I know exactly what I want to do, Keil. I have only one thing to say to them."

She leaned closer to the ear she held tightly and spoke clearly.

"Hey, asshole. Shift."

Epilogue

"She really made them shift?"

TJ, Tad and a few other close friends of Keil's sat together in one of the side rooms of the hall waiting for Robyn to appear. She was still getting ready for their entrance as the new Alphas for the pack and her first full moon.

"Oh, not only that, she made them stand around and introduce themselves. Butt naked in the cold. Then they had to apologize to us both for 'disturbing the serenity of our honeymoon'." Keil watched the ladies room door anxiously, adjusting the medallion around his neck again. If she didn't show up soon, he'd go pull her out. "I thought Jack was going to pop a vein when she suggested he might like to look into purchasing one of the penis enhancers they advertise online."

Tad choked on his drink. "My sister?"

Keil exchanged knowing glances with TJ. "Oh, yeah. She's amazing. Don't piss her off any more than you usually do. Now that she's full wolf she's a bit of a handful."

Tad sat back and swallowed hard. Keil grinned at him. "Wait until she starts ordering you around."

"Are you getting me in trouble out there, Keil?"

He turned to face the door, eager for her to arrive. *"Of course not. You can get yourself in trouble all by yourself once you get here. Are you planning on arriving any time this century?"*

Scuffling noises on the other side of the door made him more hopeful than her words. *"Look, oh tall and buff one, you only told me tonight there was going to be streaking involved in this shinding. I had to do a little more grooming than usual. Are you sure I have to get naked?"*

The door opened and Robyn stepped through, dressed in a pale blue robe. Her hair swung loose over her shoulders and her eyes seemed to glow with the reflected light of the moon.

Keil's heart rose up and choked off his throat. The scent of her wolf increased as the moon drew nearer. This is what he'd been waiting for all his life.

"Oh, yeah. You definitely have to get naked."

Desire rolled over both of them as they stared into each other's eyes, the rest of the people in the room forgotten.

"Gag." TJ pretended to slip his finger down his throat. He slid in front of Robyn and kissed her cheek. "While I'm glad you're going to be my sister-in-law and my Alpha, can you save the sex for when you get in front of the pack?"

Robyn's face went completely white as she whipped around to glare at Keil. *"Is there any tiny, insignificant detail that you might have forgotten to inform me about tonight?"*

He shrugged and gave a look to let her know how much he wanted her. *"It may have slipped my mind. But I don't think you'll mind too much. We'll be wolves. It's time to go."*

He turned and offered his arm to lead her into the moonlight of the clearing. Robyn paused for a second and Keil offered up a prayer she wouldn't go too ballistic on him.

Shaking her head, she laid a hand on his elbow and walked with a regal air through the door into the main hall with him.

"I need to do something special for you. A surprise since you obviously like them. Oh, I know. I'm making you a big batch of

brownies tomorrow. Just for you. With 'special' ingredients."

She leaned over and kissed his cheek, then whispered in his ear. "And you're going to eat them all."

Keil stopped them for a moment as they approached the center of the gathering. He stared into her eyes, seeing the twinkle of mischief overtaking the anger. She was amazing, this mate of his. Just what he needed in his life and what the pack needed as well.

He released her arm and turned to face her. Carefully crossing his hands over his heart he dipped his head. *"I love you, little bird. Shall we go become Alpha?"*

"With you, anything."

"Good. You get to share the brownies."

Wolf Flight

Dedication

To Jess Dee and Rhian Cahill and Mari Carr. You've taught me, encouraged me and cheered for me. I've been so fortunate to share this adventure with such amazing writers.

To the rest of *International Heat.* Joy, Jambrea, Valerie, Lila and Theresa. We may be spread around the world, but I never feel like you're more than a hug away.

As always to my hubby, my source of endless location inspiration. We need another trip down the Yukon River. Soon.

Chapter One

September, Whistler, British Columbia

The Whistler pack house was crowded after dinner, with small groups gathered around the room talking amongst themselves. Conversations quieted for a moment as laughter burst out from where the Alpha and his cronies sat in the prime seats before the huge stone fireplace. An icy warning trickled up Missy's spine, and she gave up on the discussion in front of her. She rose from her chair and headed quietly toward the exit, weaving between the couches and recliners that filled the meeting and relaxation area for the pack.

Missy had no illusions about the precariousness of her position. As the widow of a high-ranking wolf, even one whose position had come from his family relationship instead of his power, she was an obvious target for any of the wolves looking to improve their standing in the pack.

Which would be, oh, pretty much everyone. Only she wasn't worried about all of them, just one very dangerous individual.

It could have been worse. It *would* have been worse if she hadn't managed to keep her secret. Hidden her developing skills away not only from her late husband but the rest of them.

Even now her Alpha's gaze burned as she walked with her head down, attempting to remain small and unnoticeable as she slipped through the common area toward her apartment at the back of the complex.

“Missy,” Doug called. “Come here.”

She turned toward him, the hair on the back of her neck standing upright as a shiver of disgust raced over her skin. She had hoped to avoid this summons for far longer. Stopping a polite distance away to stand before the massive fireplace, Missy clutched her fingers together and averted her eyes at the last second.

“Jeff has been gone for a month now,” he noted, his long well-groomed fingers tapping on the arm of the overstuffed leather chair. His stylish business suit, clean-shaven chin and immaculately groomed hair sharply contrasted with what she knew of his personality. She’d seen his wolf kill more often than necessary, even for an Alpha trying to maintain order in a large pack.

Missy rocked on her feet uneasily. Doug rose from his seat to tower over her petite frame, the heat from his body close enough to overwhelm the fire’s warmth. She stared away from him, looking over the heads of the wolves sprawled on the couch immediately in front of them. *Don’t let him know how much you loathe him. Don’t show any sign of disrespect.* Others in the room looked on with curiosity for a minute before turning back to their own conversations. Only the wolf enforcers she spotted scattered inconspicuously throughout the room tensed, ready to spring into action if needed.

The level of paranoia her Alpha encouraged among his warriors shocked her. Did they really think she would challenge Doug? It seemed few pack members were aware he was less than the honourable businessman he pretended to be. Missy wondered how much the Alpha shared with his closest allies, how many of his wrongdoings the other leaders of the pack approved. Or were the Beta and the rest ignorant victims as well?

"Does it bother you to hear me talk about my brother? Do you miss him that much?" Doug's refined voice prickled in her ears. "I didn't think you pined for his conversation or longed for his arms to hold you at night."

He laughed softly and the sound grated on her nerves like nails on a blackboard. Over the past couple years Missy had become aware of slow changes in her abilities, including an increased sense of others' motivations. The evil Doug delved into permeated every fiber of his being, and Missy turned her head away to avoid showing her disgust. She swallowed hard and forced down the emotions that threatened to engulf her. Her anger, her fear. The almost overwhelming desire to turn and flee from his presence.

She couldn't run, not yet. She needed more time. Time to find an escape from the trap she knew closed around her as each day passed.

Doug ran a finger down her cheek, plucking at a blonde curl, and her gorge rose. Missy concentrated on presenting a calm façade, forcing her eyes to blink naturally as she slowed her pulse, her breathing. Calming all the telltale signs that could alert this powerful werewolf of her intentions.

He was her brother-in-law, her Alpha, but she refused to let him control her. The finger continued a slow path down her body as she stood stock-still.

"Jeff never did know what a treasure he had, did he?" Doug asked, his dark voice dirty like an oily slick over her skin. He leaned close to whisper in her ear. "My sweet Omega."

Her eyes flickered for a split second before she tamped down the surprise. How could he have discovered what she had worked so hard to hide? She was still learning to control her untrained skills, including the ability to read and manipulate others' emotions, to calm and ease them. Omegas were rare and highly desired among the shifter community. With appropriate guidance, she would be a blessing to a pack. Under the wrong influence, her skills could be deadly.

There were no doubts in Missy's mind what kind of leadership headed her pack at the present time.

Doug chuckled, a light sound that nevertheless made her skin crawl. "Oh, yes, I know. I've always known. You can't hide potential ability from an Alpha who's looking for it." He flicked a finger over his head and the wolves seated around them dispersed, conversations fading away to leave them intimately alone. Missy's fear tripled and icy fingers crawled up her spine in spite of the fire blazing at her back.

Doug lifted her chin with a thick finger, tilting her face as if he were examining a side of beef at the butcher's. He snorted and spoke softly, his words for her alone. "When I blackmailed your family into your marriage to my brother, I hoped you would end up permanently linked with him. With a mate connection between you, I would have mastered you both. But like everything else Jeff touched, he ruined my plans. He wasn't even strong enough to trap you with a false FirstMate."

Missy shuddered inside at the thought. Like every wolf she longed to find her mate, the one who matched her not only physically but emotionally. Forced into a loveless marriage to save her family had been bad enough, but it would have been far worse to imagine herself belonging body, mind and soul to Jeff simply because of overactive pheromones.

A strong hand wrapped around her neck, pulling her closer as Doug stared, his nostrils flaring as he examined her face minutely. "He was woefully delinquent in training you to be obedient. But he's gone now, that unfortunate incident, you know."

Missy's heart thumped harder as the truth of the accident flowed involuntarily from Doug's mind to hers. Images flashed—

ropes cut by knives, a falling body, triggered rock falls—she blinked slowly, carefully. The information transferred between them as clearly as if he had spoken, the knowledge a gift and curse of being an Omega wolf.

His own brother had killed her husband. Closing her eyes to shut out the pain, she forced her tears to remain hidden. She may not have loved Jeff, but he hadn't deserved to die in that manner. The crackle of the fire sounded loud and eerie as she searched for something to concentrate on to clear her mind of Doug's filthy touch.

Doug grunted. "Hmmm, you are good. So much potential, so much I'll be able to do with you once you're properly trained." Doug loosened his grip for a second and slipped his fingers into her hair, tugging it hard enough to bring tears to her eyes.

Her blood pounded, her mouth suddenly gone dry, and she focused on making Doug forget her. She was nothing, she was nondescript. Reaching deep into the part of herself she had hidden away for years, she attempted to calm her Alpha. The ripping pull in her hair faded as he dropped his hands to his side and released her.

She kept her gaze on his face and continued to pour out calming emotions from her core, being sure to make them nonthreatening, noninteresting. Above all nonsexual because if Doug decided to claim her physically she'd be lost. She would shatter in a million pieces and never be free from him.

He turned away from her and her panic lightened, fear relaxing as he reacted to her stimulus. She drew in an uneven breath, preparing to step back and retreat from his presence. Suddenly, his hand shot out and wrapped around her throat, squeezing tight enough to hurt and she froze, physically and mentally. He snarled quietly. "Don't attempt your tricks, little girl. You're strong, much stronger than my brother was, so you were able to control him. Don't make the mistake of assuming you can use your skills on me. I *will* kill you if you try that again." He squeezed a final time before releasing her, his hand moving to cup her face as she frantically dragged in air.

His voice was a mere whisper, menacing in its softness, the polite trappings of civilization hiding the monster. "I'm a patient man, Missy. I waited until the opportune moment to take over the pack. I have maneuvered tirelessly to arrange deals that will soon bring in the financial resources I desire. I can wait for you until the timing is right. Since appearances are so important to wolves, I wouldn't dream of taking you yet. I don't want to draw any attention from the council. Even though you obviously are hurting, missing your mate." His fingers trailed along her cheek and she shivered involuntarily. "Poor thing, everyone knows how devastating it is to lose a mate. It is fortunate I'm without a partner. As both Alpha and your brother-in-law, I'm the only one who can replace him for you."

He dropped his hand away, sliding it intimately down her body.

If she had truly been mated, Doug's words would have been true. The loss of a mate ripped something from within, and many never recovered. With the genetic similarities between brothers, and Doug's strength as an Alpha, the pack would expect him to take Missy under his protection.

And into his bed.

Only she and Jeff hadn't been mates. There had been no true connection between them other than a shared zeal to stay alive under the tyranny of an Alpha who controlled and conquered as he pleased. Jeff hadn't survived.

She stiffened her spine, glancing into the common room to see if there was anyone nearby even watching the discussion that she might turn to for assistance. No one paid them any attention. A log popped and shifted at her back, a rush of heat flaring out and she took a deep breath. It was up to her alone.

Missy was desperate to escape, but Doug still held power over her. Still held her in check with the one thing that guaranteed her cooperation. She needed time to find a way to get out of this mess. “I'm scheduled to leave the pack for an extended period of time. My position with the research team has been—”

Doug waved a hand in front of her face. “I know. You'll be traveling with the Lauren Group setting up weather stations. I believe the timeframe is four to five months for the work to be completed, correct?”

Missy swore inside. How could the bastard know the details of a personal contract she'd signed only days ago? She'd attempted to be extremely careful in keeping her information secretive, but his fingers were in everything.

“I will expect you by the end of February.” His dark eyes flashed at her. “Don't make the mistake of delaying your return, Missy, or there will be consequences your sister will not enjoy.”

She stood rigid under his glare. “Leave Margaret out of this. She's attending university in Vancouver, she's not a part of this pack anymore.”

Doug shook his head. “No one is truly ever out from the protective watch of the pack, you should know that. I'm sure Maggie will be just fine as long as you remember your place in the overall scheme of things.” He leaned close and brushed his lips against her cheek, whispering in her ear, “Six months, my little Omega. I'll give you six months as the code states. Then I'm taking you as mine and our combined skills will be the making of this pack.” He dismissed her abruptly, turning away to reclaim his chair, glittering eyes staring into the fire.

The enforcers gathered around Doug again as Missy backed away, eager to leave the sweltering heat that had nothing to do with the blaze in the fireplace. She forced herself to walk, not run, head held high. No indication that the devil himself had just announced she was to be his queen.

There was no way she would willingly join him in hell.

Chapter Two

February, Haines Junction, Yukon

Tad leaned against the cold exterior wall as he watched the company helicopter settle on the runway. Loose snow flew around the large metal-clad building they used as a hangar for both the chopper and the small bush plane. He waved briefly at his business partner, Shaun, before hurrying back indoors. There wasn't much time left and he had a ton of preparations to complete before the afternoon flight.

Maxwell's Silver Hammer had landed a major contract to transport researchers to and from a camp at the base of Mount Logan. The money was great but the timing sucked. As he hurried through his checklist his mind wandered, concern for his sister distracting him. What the *hell* was he thinking, letting a deaf girl head into the backcountry alone? He was supposed to take care of her, not throw her to the wolves. He should have refused the contract and gone with her like they originally planned. He was lost in thought when a solid touch to his shoulder startled him.

"Holy shit, Shaun, warn a guy will you?" Tad cursed, his heart racing.

"You're a fucking werewolf. Why the hell can't you learn to scent another wolf approaching?" Shaun peeled off his flight jacket and threw it onto one of the chairs at the side of the shop. His cocky grin did little to relax the knot in Tad's stomach.

"Piss off." So his ability to smell sucked. There were more important things to worry about as far as he was concerned. "Robyn get away okay? Crap, I can't believe I let her go on the trip without me. What if something happens to her?"

Shaun laughed, slapping him on the back roughly. "You're too damn possessive about your sister. She's fine. She's a great skier and experienced in the bush. Plus she's so freaking powerful that being stuck in close quarters with her nearly kills me." He paused for a second, flicking a concerned glance at Tad. "You've got to tell her soon. I mean, you've known about having werewolf genes for a couple of years now. She needs to know so she can move on with her life, learn about her other side. She's going to be the most gorgeous wolf when she gets her genes triggered."

Tad grit his teeth together, his face suddenly hot, muscles tense. *Not this conversation again.* "Yeah, and I suppose you want the privilege of triggering her, right?"

Shaun wiggled his eyebrows a few times and grinned. "Well, it wouldn't be a chore by any stretch."

Tad slammed a hand into his friend's chest, hooked his fingers into his shirt and lifted him off his feet. Blood pounded in his ears and Tad looked out through a sea of red. Shaun's toes dangled off the ground, kicking a few times as Tad held him high in the air, arm stretched at full length.

"Shit, Tad, I'm kidding around. Put me down." Shaun wiggled, his face suddenly gone white.

Fuck.

Tad dropped Shaun to the ground and reached up to pinch the bridge of his nose. "Sorry, I'm feeling a little stressed. Between Robyn and the booking and my skin itching like it's going to crawl off and walk on its own..."

Shaun moved away cautiously, tugging his clothes straight. "For an untriggered wolf, you're too damn strong. I don't know which is worse, your bark or your bite. The itching is your wolf trying to get out. You need to get triggered soon because you and Robyn are both missing a huge part of your lives—"

"Are you her mate?"

"No, but—"

"Then keep your fucking hands off her."

Shaun backed down, keeping his body language submissive. "Maybe you should give her the choice. Tell her she's got werewolf genes and let her decide what to do about it."

Tad collapsed into a chair, his body sprawled back in a messy heap. Discovering werewolves existed had been like crossing into the Twilight Zone. Finding out both he and his adopted sister had the genes necessary to be able to turn into wolves had been even more of a surprise. But the rest of the details drove him insane. "Shit, I've started to tell her a dozen times but just thinking about it makes me sweat. Why the heck does it have to be sex that triggers the gene in adults? Like I want to tell my sister to go fuck someone. Robyn has enough on her plate being deaf. She doesn't need the drama of trying to find a mate as well. Plus I can't shift to prove anything until I get triggered myself."

He closed his eyes and scrubbed at his face in frustration. "You were lucky. My parents don't know anything about wolves. My grandpa must have provided the genes and then died before telling anyone his secret. You were born into a full-blood family and got triggered from your mom's milk, so it wasn't like you had a dire need for sex."

Shaun snorted. "Not a dire need? Shit, don't you remember what it's like to be a teenager?"

"Horny bastard. And you wonder why I want you to stay away from Robyn," Tad complained, his anger slipping away although his frustration remained high. Shaun didn't seem to understand how aggravating it was for Tad as a half-blood. He needed a hormone trigger too, only his would be released the first time he had sex with a female wolf. Tad liked sex as much as the next guy, but the human females he'd been with didn't count. There was one final catch kicking him in the ass, making it damn near impossible to get triggered.

Bloody wolf hormones.

"Doesn't it bother you?" Tad asked. "Being out of control of your own destiny?"

"What are you talking about?"

"The wolf. The way being a wolf changes your whole life." Tad stared into space, his fingers fidgeting with the arms of his chair.

Shaun scrunched up his face. "Uh, no... I mean, so I can change into a wolf. It's no big deal. It's not like I have uncontrollable urges to howl or shift involuntarily when the moon is full. My wolf is just a part of who I am. An amazing, completely honest part of me."

Tad snorted. "You've never been so poetic in your life. Damn it, I'm talking about the stupid wolf hormones. Don't try to tell me they don't dictate your life. They sure as hell do mine. We can't even decide who to marry without our wolves approving."

His partner laughed as he leaned back on the table. "Mates? You're worried about finding a mate again, Tad? Holy crap, you need to get laid."

"I know that, you asshole."

Shaun shook his head. "Not just to trigger your genes, brainiac. To relax. Find yourself a nice human girl and have at it. You haven't gone out with anyone for months. You need to let your wolf out to play." He nabbed a picture off the wall behind him and waved it at Tad, his grin growing larger by the second. "What about your dream girl? She'll be in town soon, won't she?"

Tad leapt up and snatched the photo away. "Leave Missy out of this. She's special." Shaun rocked his eyebrows up and down, and Tad flipped him the bird as he replaced the picture, tracing the edge with a finger. "She's not a wolf, so I refuse to mess around with her."

"Holy shit, are you telling me you've only fucked women you might marry?"

"No, but…crap! See, this is what I mean. I like Missy. I really like her and always have. If I wasn't a wolf I'd be interested in spending time with her to see if something develops between us. But since my damn wolf decides my partner, I have no bloody choice in the matter. I don't think it's fair to string along a human woman."

Tad waved a hand in frustration at Shaun and returned to his preparations. It was quiet in the hangar, both of them working silently, deep in thought. He did like Missy. It had been a complete surprise when she'd contacted him by email. Over the past four months, they'd been corresponding back and forth about life in general, catching up on the years they'd been apart.

The day she wrote about her husband and his death, Tad had gone for a long run, pushing himself to the point of exhaustion. He wondered why it pissed him off so much to discover she'd cared enough for someone else to make a lifetime commitment with him. Heck, he and Missy had never been lovers. They'd barely held hands as teenagers back in high school before she'd moved south.

Shaun leaned on the side of the plane next to where Tad

was working, his dark eyes crinkled up with concern. "I'm sorry things haven't worked out faster for you. It'll be worth it in the end, really it will."

Tad sighed and thumped his partner's shoulder. Shaun's heart was in the right place. "It's just I've tried for two years to follow wolf rules and it's gotten me nowhere. As much as I want to be able to shift, I don't know if I can live like this much longer. I can't change my morals to turn wolf."

Shaun nodded sadly. "I understand. But you're not going to be really happy until you get triggered."

Tad returned to his adjustments. "Yeah, well, in the meantime I've got you to piss me off and help me let off steam." He stared hard at his friend. "I want forever someday. I believe in true love and finding my other half. I know it's romantic shit, but I still believe in it."

"Yeah, I hear you, but until you find Ms. Right, I really think you should consider Ms. Right Now."

✧

Missy took a deep breath, looking around the small airfield with interest while she let the butterflies settle. Her journey over the past months had led her in a full circle, returning her to old stomping grounds. She'd grown up in Whitehorse, lived in the north until she was sixteen. How strange the solution to the horror hanging over her head might be found here.

She stared at the doors to the shop.

Ten years.

Ten years since she'd seen Tad, one of the most intriguing boys she'd ever met. He'd been a grade above her in high school and she'd liked him intensely, even though her father had insisted half-blood Tad be avoided and not informed of his wolf heritage. Missy had reluctantly followed her father's rules and never let herself be alone with Tad. Never accepted any of his hesitant physical advances beyond public hugs and cuddles during movie marathons. Only participated in group activities.

Something had always felt missing. She'd longed for more.

Slipping in the door, Missy took in the neat and tidy waiting area, the newspaper clippings taped to the wall. She moved closer to examine the articles about Maxwell's Silver Hammer, providers of "custom sightseeing flights, fishing charters and all-round *you want to get lost in the wilderness, we'll get you there* services". Pictures accompanying the articles showed the helicopter she'd seen outside and a small plane outfitted with skis or water floats.

A brightly coloured strip of paper caught her eye and she bent to examine it.

A metallic clang hit the floor behind her, and she spun around to see a tall, wiry hunk staring with lust in his eyes. Confusion clouded the dark orbs for a moment before recognition hit.

"Missy?"

Her heart leapt. His tone of voice made her very glad she'd decided to deal with her problem by seeking him out.

She beamed at him. "Hello, Tad." She tilted her head toward the articles. "You told me business was going well but you didn't say how well. Glowing reports from what I see here."

She held out her hand, and when he clasped it, she tucked herself under his arm and hugged him tightly, his body cradling hers carefully. She took a cautious sniff as she held him. His scent was familiar yet somehow his wolf was muted, which was curious. She didn't smell any females on him and that was a good thing.

A very good thing, considering what she had in mind.

"It really is wonderful to see you again." She clung to him for another second, relaxing in his strong arms. It felt so right to be held by another wolf, especially one not threatening to kill her. She hadn't dared raise the issue during their email correspondence, but she needed to know. Was he aware of his wolf heritage? Opening her mind, she reached out tentatively to brush his emotions. Images jumped back—her face during a high school event, sliding down a snow-covered hill together, the view of her butt as she bent over moments earlier by the door—and she smiled. Nothing but memories filled his mind. Tad gave a final squeeze before extending her to an arm's distance.

"Damn, you look incredible. I mean, I got the picture you sent but you're so..." Tad stared, his gaze trailing over her face in amazement.

Missy sighed. The petite thing didn't help. "I know. I look like a teenager. I'm twenty-six and I still get IDed every time I order a drink."

Tad led her to the customer waiting area and gestured toward the couch. He hesitated for a second before slipping into the chair across from her. Missy dropped her head to keep her smile hidden. She couldn't help noticing his arousal. Both his body and his scent gave him away.

"It's great to see you, but I wasn't expecting you until next week." He slid a hand through his hair leaving the dark spikes a mess. Missy wanted to drag her own fingers through the strands and wondered what he would do if she reached out and gave in to temptation. He glanced at his watch and fidgeted. "I don't want to be rude. I mean, I've been looking forward to your visit, but I've got a customer this afternoon and I'm not finished prepping. Do you mind if I slip out back for a bit? It should only take ten minutes."

Missy frowned. Hadn't he figured it out? She was sure

she'd told him the reason she'd come north. Or while trying to be secretive about other things, had she forgotten? "Tad, I have an appointment."

He let out a big sigh, sounding relieved as he pulled her to her feet and gently tugged her back toward the door. "That's great! Why don't you go get your stuff done first and then come back and meet me in half an hour? We can visit until my customers get here."

"But—" She was out the door, back into the bright and cool February day.

"Looking forward to it. Sorry, I've got to hustle. See you later."

Tad closed the door behind her and Missy stared in shock. She burst out laughing as she made her way back to her truck. *That had gone splendidly. Not!* She giggled, delighted at the lightness of her mood. There had been little to laugh about over the past months and this mixed-up situation was her fault. She'd dressed to impress. It obviously worked based on his physical reaction, but he was a little too distracted.

She reached into the cab of the truck and grabbed her work clothes. It looked like her excuse for coming to the Yukon would be needed after all.

Chapter Three

Tad raced back into the shop area, scrambling to finish rigging the webbing for the afternoon flight. It was hard to fit the snaps together with visions of Missy flitting through his brain.

Missy. He'd been totally in love with her from the first minute he'd seen her, all blonde, blue-eyed and mischievous. He'd wanted to scoop her up and eat her in one bite, but in high school he'd been even shier with girls than he was now.

What he'd told Shaun was true. He didn't feel right fooling around with Missy since there wasn't going to be a future for them. But, *holy crap*, did she turn his crank. Something about her made him burn inside, and she wasn't even trying.

He had almost finished his tasks when the door chime ran again.

"I'll be with you in a minute," he shouted toward the front office. "Grab a coffee if you'd like." He hurried to tighten the last few straps.

"I don't drink coffee."

Tad swung around. The pale pink down-filled coat, the skintight leggings and the beautiful long blonde hair that hung in fat ringlets were all gone. In their place Missy wore a shapeless woolen toque complete with large earflaps and a generic one-piece blue jumpsuit with a stylized badge on her chest stating “LRG” in bold yellow letters.

“Missy?”

She held up a hand to silence him, then rotated. On the back of her suit the bright yellow words “Lauren Research Group” jumped out at Tad.

Oh shit.

She finished her spin and stared at him, face blank and unreadable.

Tad swallowed hard. He’d really put his foot in it this time.

She crossed her arms and leaned back as she glared up at him. “Hi, I’m Ms. Leason. I’m the representative from LRG you agreed to fly to the set-up site this afternoon, and I’d like your permission to prepack the boxes.”

“I’m sorry. I was so distracted by seeing you earlier it never occurred to me you could be from LRG. Not that there’s any reason why you couldn’t be from LRG.” He wasn’t sure where to look because even in that damn coverall she made his body twitch. And wasn’t that just what he needed, to have his mouth full of feet and his balls in a knot.

She held up her hand again, tilting her head to the side as she raised one eyebrow. “This means you volunteer to help me pack *and* you’re buying me dinner. Right?” She smirked at him as she pulled off the toque and the riot of hair fell around her. “Holy cow, you should see your face. I thought you might pass out there for a minute.”

Tad swept his hand through his hair and pulled his jaw off the floor. “You, oh man. Yeah, you’re right. I almost lost it. Missy, I’m sorry I cut you off.”

Missy waved a hand in the air. “It’s okay. It wasn’t fair of me to let you assume I’d simply dropped by to see you. I thought I’d mentioned working for LRG in our emails but I guess not. No harm done, but I’m serious about needing help with the gear."

Tad shook his finger at her, taking in her bright expression. "You always were a bad one for teasing." He turned away to swing open the doors of the four-seater plane and rolled the portable steps into place. "What are you transporting that's so delicate?"

"They're not delicate but my job will be easier if they get packed in order. The relays for the weather sensors need to be set in sequence. I'd prefer not to have to spend hours sorting while we're on the mountainside. Everything is in the transport trailer outside."

Tad pulled open the overhead hangar doors and let out a long whistle. Missy drove a brand-new long-box Toyota extra-crew cab with matching canopy. "Sweet wheels."

He peeked in the window of the passenger door to admire the interior. Behind him Missy released a big sigh. "Boys and their toys. Yes, it's a nice truck. It starts when I turn the key, and both the radio and CD player work so I'm happy. Oh, and it's bright red. Makes it easy to spot in the parking lot."

They grinned at each other. Damn, he loved a girl with a sense of humour. Tad raised his eyebrows, flashing her the best puppy-dog eyes he could. "You want me to move it?" Backing the attached twenty-five-foot trailer into the open space in the hangar would be a hellish task.

"No, I'll drive. Should I park next to the plane?"

Tad opened his mouth to protest but managed to stop himself in time. He prided himself on being a quick learner. He wouldn't assume anything about the golden goddess in front of him from this point on because apparently Missy was a woman of many talents.

"By the plane is fine. I'll get the steps out of your way."

He strolled back to the plane, watching Missy over his

shoulder as she crawled up into the cab. She did a funny little hop to get in the seat and he wondered how she reached the gas pedal and still saw out the window.

She pulled the truck and trailer out of his line of vision into the main parking lot and then in one smooth move reversed in. Tad shook his head. He would have needed at least three attempts to get that monster of a rig to back into the tight space.

He'd spent years adoring Missy-the-girl in high school. Missy-the-woman got more and more interesting by the minute.

Missy jumped down and rubbed her hands together briskly, her delighted smile showing she'd noticed his admiration. "How do you want to do this? The boxes are all lined up and just need to be kept in order."

Tad opened the side doors of the trailer. "You crawl in the plane and place them where you want them. I'll be your Sherpa." A faint scent tickled his nose and his heartbeat sped up. She must be wearing a killer perfume for *him* to be able to smell it. He tried to ignore his body's response because he needed to keep this professional. Businesslike. Her long hair brushed his skin as he helped her into the storage section of the plane, and his cock leapt to attention.

So much for keeping things calm.

He hurried to fetch the first load of boxes, trying to pretend there wasn't a baseball bat stuck in his pants.

They chatted easily as they worked, picking up their online conversation from the previous week. It was incredible to be with Missy after all these years and hear her laugh, watch her face light up as she spoke. She'd changed so little. She still looked like the sweet girl of sixteen that he'd fallen for, but there was a shadow that passed over her eyes now and then. Was it the loss of her husband that put the darkness into her sparkling personality?

Physically she knocked his knees out from under him. Mentally and emotionally, she tied him in knots. Memories had poured through his brain since the first second he'd recognized her. Memories and longings he'd put aside in his quest to become a wolf. He had to be careful not to let his physical attraction make him do anything he'd regret. This was one woman he refused to hurt above all others.

"Do you like Whistler?" he asked, trying to head the conversation back into neutral territory. His erection eased as they worked, the returning blood flow to his brain making it easier to concentrate. "I have some friends who go skiing there every year, but I haven't heard much about the community."

She hesitated for a surprisingly long time before answering. "The mountains are glorious and I enjoy being in a small town again after living in Vancouver. It's not the Yukon though. There's something special about the north I've missed."

Tad reached to give her hand a reassuring squeeze. The touch of skin on skin was like grabbing a live wire. Energy flowed between them sending small shocks up his arm. He jerked his fingers away. "Shoot. The static electricity is crazy in here."

Missy had the strangest expression on her face. She held a hand to Tad. "Try again."

Tad hesitated and then clasped fingers. This time the energy didn't snap but it was there, a low buzz of tingles spreading over him.

It felt good.

Too good. Tad pulled away before parts of his anatomy he didn't want to reawaken heard the alarm ringing through him. "What's that all about?" he asked in confusion.

Missy shook her head. "I'm not sure. Maybe like you said—static electricity. Some people are better conductors than others."

"Weird." Tad turned away to get the next set of boxes. His whole body was hot, and he had the strange desire to pick Missy up and carry her back to his apartment and ravish her until they were both so sated neither of them could move. Well, okay, it wasn't a completely unexpected emotion since she was pretty easy on the eyes, and he'd always had a huge crush on her. Yet he'd never had an attack of the hormone kind this hard before. It was unsettling, especially when he wanted to impress Missy, not come across like some northern Neanderthal.

Gotta stay calm. Cool.

"How's your sister?" Missy asked.

Tad leapt at the change in topic. "She's gone bush this week for a getaway. I was supposed to go with her but had to cancel. Shaun, my business partner, insists she'll be just fine but I'm still concerned. I know she's strong but since I found out..." Tad coughed suddenly, frantic to cover up that he had nearly told Missy about being a wolf. He must be tired because he had *never* slipped like that before.

It was Shaun's fault for getting him thinking about having sex with a human woman right before the biggest wet dream of his life walked through the door. He glanced at where she sat in the open storage compartment of the plane, her feet dangling in midair. Curls draped over her shoulders, the ugly coverall unable to hide the curves of her petite frame. A shot of lust raced through him. Damn, he couldn't blame this on Shaun. It was his own body jerking him around. He was horny and a total bastard all on his own.

Missy seemed deep in thought and Tad fought a case of wandering hands. The need to touch her was so bad it made his whole body hurt. Missy gave him one of her shy smiles. "I'm sure Robyn will be fine. She always was extremely independent."

He hurried to reassure her. “I know, I just like to worry. It comes with the territory.”

They stared at each other.

Missy looked away first, biting her lower lip. Tad shut his mouth tight so the groan that wanted to escape was locked away. Everything about Missy called for him to step forward and—

She grabbed the front of his shirt and tugged until he stood between her legs, their torsos nestled together. Lips, soft and warm, brushed his, that strange electric sensation enveloping his body at the same time. Tad pulled Missy closer and kissed back, nibbling her lips, caressing the curve of her cheek with small touches. He snuck a hand into her curls and cupped her head to direct her mouth to the right angle to enjoy her fully.

She opened her lips and he tasted her for the first time. Sweet and spicy, intoxicating.

Addictive.

His tongue made a tentative dip into her mouth, a brief stroke against hers, then retreated as they explored the newness of the kiss. What he’d imagined as a teenager was nothing like the experience as an adult.

Heat rose between them as his body reacted to Missy’s softness. Tad fought to keep his hands loose around her instead of trapping her against the plane like he wanted to. He forced himself to kiss her instead of feasting on her lips, forced himself to let the sweetness of the experience flow over them like a fine wine.

They separated at the same moment, fingers linked together even as their lips parted. Tad stared into Missy’s eyes and saw his need reflected back.

Sweet mercy, she wanted him too.

Tad leaned forward, ready to recapture her lips when she

pressed a hand against his chest.

"We need to finish. The others could be here anytime."

Deep breath.

Tad nodded. He dropped one final kiss on her mouth, a fleeting brush of lips, the promise of more. Simply touching her made his body ache. There was no way he could deny the attraction between them. It was time he made up his mind, and right now his wolf side was losing the battle. Waiting to find forever with a wolf mate was one choice, but perhaps he could find forever in a different direction.

✧

Alone in her hotel room that night Missy paced, unable to sit still with the energy surging through her. The day had turned out nothing like she expected. She still felt Tad's mouth on hers, the caress of his hands on her body. Never before had she experienced such a strong attraction. The connection with Tad was overpowering, a little frightening and divinely potent. Was it what she wanted?

Was it what she needed?

After fleeing Whistler she had worked days and researched at night until nearly a month later she found a possible solution to her problem.

Wolf hormones.

The genetic differences between werewolves and humans were small but profound. It was the presence of unique chemicals that made possible the physical transformation between forms. Those same compounds caused the incredible bond between wolf couples to occur. The creation of lifetime mates was a blessing, but there was a hidden curse. Male wolves built up an excess supply of the hormones during adolescence.

While wolves and humans could have sex, the chemicals were only released during intimacy with a female wolf. A cousin once told Missy guys jokingly called the situation "double virginity". No matter how active their sex life with humans, males still had to lose their wolf virginity with a female more powerful than them or the huge amount of hormones released could backfire, creating a pheromone overload.

The female would become hopelessly obsessed with her partner due to nothing more than a chemical chain reaction. A false mate, with the lifetime connection on only one side.

That was how her brother-in-law had hoped to gain control over her. Doug thought compelling Missy into marriage with his inexperienced brother would trap her.

Missy opened the window to let in the cold night air, the room suddenly close and unbearable. She leaned her head against the windowsill, fighting down the shudders that threatened to overtake her as she remembered her wedding night. It wasn't the sex that had scared her, but she hadn't been in love and her terror of becoming trapped had made the experience hell. Missy had always considered it a miracle she was a stronger wolf than anyone expected.

And now she discovered an overload would not only have forced a false mate, the destructive chemical reaction would have also eliminated her latent Omega talents.

She resumed pacing, the small space of the hotel room like a cage around her. The solution had been there all the time. Wolf society knew about false mates and had guidelines in the code to help prevent it. They had even developed the ritual of FirstMate once it was discovered that if a male's first experience was with a wolf who was already mated, the chemicals had no effect.

If she could provide FirstMate to a powerful wolf, it could

destroy her talents and she would be free. Doug would have no use for her without intact Omega abilities. Giving up a part of herself to avoid being used as a tool seemed an acceptable sacrifice. Even if it meant she would forever love someone who didn't love her back.

But who should she approach to offer FirstMate? Only strong wolves or mated females with their husband's approval could offer to act as a guide. In her case it would be assumed as a widow she would be safe from the hormone backlash. If the attempt failed she had decided she would shift into her wolf and disappear from human society forever. The Yukon was a logical safe haven. Her time was running out and if FirstMate didn't work, going feral seemed the only choice left.

And Tad was in the north. Missy had always remembered him and his face was the first to rush to her mind, perhaps for a good reason. They had only kept their hands off each other during the afternoon's work because the crew from LRG joined them. Was it possible that she was already reacting to a false mating? Just from a kiss?

Did Tad know he had wolf genes? She couldn't let him make love to her and then leave him to face a world for which he wasn't prepared. Because he was a half-blood, having sex with her would trigger his wolf, and by the next full moon he would be able to shift. He needed to be warned, trained, and she wouldn't be here after their rendezvous. She would either return to Whistler to prove her skills were gone or she would disappear into the wilderness.

Missy forced herself to stop daydreaming about Tad. There were other goals yet to accomplish. Opening her laptop she logged into the first stage of the Whistler-wolf-pack website. Maggie was still online. Her sister's habitual evening online chat was their prearranged set-up. It gave Missy information she would never be able to access otherwise. When Maggie signed out at nine p.m., Missy entered her sister's pass code with a false ISP number and snuck into the system while the time clock stayed motionless. Missy took a big breath and blew it out in a slow stream. The records would continue to show her sister's presence until the mandatory one-hour system shutdown occurred. Missy checked her watch and set to work.

Accessing Doug's daily email records and his private message box was a piece of cake with her computer skills. She was relieved to see that while her brother-in-law continued to track her, he hadn't put out a call to make her return before her time was up and there were no plans in place to harass her sister.

Missy snooped around to gather more information on the pack's illegal activities to use as ammunition to challenge Doug. Perhaps she could leak the information to the authorities and get him arrested by the human system if the wolf council was unable to help. She did a little archive research on Omega wolf characteristics and one hour later, Missy logged out. She was still safe.

For now.

Chapter Four

Tad completed a few more official flight papers. He pulled a beer from the fridge and turned the TV on low in the background as he sat and flipped through a couple of the magazines on the table.

He was wasting time until he could go and pick up Missy for the evening and he knew it. She said she'd be ready by eight and he was fretting and worrying like he was back in high school. Three days he'd been waiting since Saturday, three nights of his mind producing the most erotic of dreams to haunt him. He had a permanent hard-on and every little glimpse of Missy at the work site simply drove his need higher.

A date with Missy, a real actual grown-up date. It was enough to make his worries about getting triggered fade into the background, at least temporarily. The phone rang and his heart leapt. Then he realized it wasn't his house phone or his cell phone.

Crap. He couldn't believe he'd forgotten about his sister. It was Tuesday and Robyn was supposed to check in tonight. Good thing he'd still been home or she would have flipped. He opened the satellite phone to check for a text message. A voice rose from the speaker instead.

Weird. Robyn never spoke out loud. She was deaf. She signed or she wrote notes or she stomped and threw things.

“Hello?” Tad said hesitantly.

“Hi, Tad, this is Keil Lynus. How are you, man?”

“Hey. I’m doing great.” He glanced down at the phone trying to figure out what was strange about this call. Keil was a regular client, a wilderness guide and a great guy who just happened to be a wolf. He was also the one who’d explained about werewolves in the first place when his little brother had screwed up and accidentally shifted in front of Tad. “What’s up? Troubles with TJ? Need help rescuing him?”

“No, TJ doesn’t need any rescuing, we already dug him out.”

“No way, I was joking. Your brother is such an ass.” Something was up. Keil never called him—he emailed his flight requests. Tad killed the sound on the TV and tried to focus.

“I know, he’s a total pain in the butt.” There was a pause for a second before Keil continued, “I do need something.”

Then it sunk in. No one should be using this number except Robyn. Tad’s stomach tightened with anxiety. Damn it, something *had* happened. “Keil? Why are you calling me on my sister’s sat phone? Is everything all right? Is she there with you or what?”

“She’s fine. In fact Robyn and I are mates, and I was—”

His stomach relaxed but all the blood in his body rushed to his head and made the room spin. *Oh my God.* “No bloody way! That’s fantastic. I never dreamed you’d be the one for her.” There were rustling sounds in the background and a couple of claps and slaps. “Is she good with it? How did she find out?”

“Hang on, Tad, she’s getting a little frisky right now. I think she’s worried you’re having a fit or something over there. Want to talk to her?”

“Of course! Just give me a second…”

Talk about astonishing news. This was better than

anything he'd ever imagined. His sister had found her mate. Too cool. He typed a message on the keypad.

Congratz sis, Keil is awesome. I'm so happy for u

U know Keil? U know what he is?

Oh yeah, he knew. *Ya. Wolf. U work fast sis*

The next message took a few seconds to arrive but he already guessed what she was going to say. It was her favourite threat. *U are sooooo dead next time I c u Tad*

luv U 2 Robyn

Jerk

Well, that seemed to be it for intelligent conversation from Robyn if she'd digressed into single word insults. The faint sound of a voice reached Tad's ears and he lifted the receiver back up to respond.

"Keil? You guys as mates? That is so cool. I mean, really." Tad was slightly shocked. Robyn had been dropped off only four days ago and they were already mates? Hell, that meant she obviously didn't have his troubles with—he shook his head. There was no way he was going to even *think* about his sister having sex.

"Well, thanks. It was a surprise but she's incredible, Tad. Hey, there is a little thing shaking down this weekend if you'd like to join us. Robyn's first full moon will be on Saturday."

Tad froze. He'd forgotten that tidbit. Now that Robyn had mated she'd be able to change into a wolf. The first shift always took place in conjuncture with the full moon to help the newbie out. Hot damn, this was exciting news. Then reality dropped like a lead balloon. "I'd love to be there but I can't shift. You know I haven't, well, I don't want to get anyone upset if it's not kosher for me to attend."

"Of course you can come! You're family, even if you aren't triggered yet."

"I mean, it's not like I don't want it to happen. I can't seem to, you know." His face grew hot, even talking about it on the phone with Keil. Full-blood wolves never seemed to understand his hesitancy to embrace FirstMate tradition.

"I know, Tad. It'll happen sometime, man. Gotta go. Robyn's making me pay for this call."

Yeah, right. Like that was an issue. "Umm, didn't you tell me you had a trust fund as well as the guiding business?"

Keil's deep voice echoed back across the line. "I know I can afford it, but why would I want to spend more time talking to you when I can be with my mate?"

Tad snickered. That sounded like Keil. "Got it. Honeymoon. Enjoy and I'll see you in Haines on Saturday. Give Robyn a kiss from me. Oh, and welcome to the family."

✧

Missy opened the door of her hotel room and flushed to see Tad extending a single yellow rose.

"Tad, how sweet. Thank you." Missy took the flower. She debated going back into the room to put it in water or leaving with it in her hand. If she went into the room she might haul Tad to the bed and never let him leave. She didn't think he was quite ready for that yet. Just because she knew he was a wolf didn't mean *he* knew he was a wolf.

Damn hormones.

"I'll go bring the truck around front. It's snowing a bit," Tad said, before winking at her and turning away.

Missy dealt with the rose and made her way to the parking lot. Tad drove a four-wheel drive that was a little older and more beat up than hers but just as high to climb into. She giggled as

Tad came to help her.

"I swear they should install elevators on these things."

Tad's hands stroked her leg as he lifted her in. "Hmmm, that's a poor idea. I'd miss getting to help the damsel in distress."

Missy held her breath while Tad trotted around the vehicle and got behind the wheel. Did he have any idea what he did to her body? Any idea how she reacted to every glance, every touch?

She snuck a quick peek at him. He seemed unaware his scent alone drove her wild. She had to be careful not to do something stupid like kiss him again or let on she was anything other than a good friend from long ago.

Who drooled at the thought of seeing him naked. There was definitely some kind of connection between them. Strong. Magnetic.

Tad concentrated on the snow-blown road. "If it's too bad out we can call tonight off," Missy offered.

"You haven't been driving in the Yukon for a while, have you?" Tad asked, a faint smile on his face. "This is great driving weather. All the tourists will stay home and we just have to look out for Old Man Henry in case he decides to go wandering after closing hours at Klondike Kate's wearing his bearskin coat. Don't worry, we'll be there soon."

Missy returned to staring at his profile as they made their way down the highway to the pub Tad insisted she needed to see. There was something different about Tad. Other than that he was an untriggered wolf. Missy had never reacted to a man like this before. He smelt different too.

Not just the different that made her mouth water, and she wasn't supposed to keep heading down *that* particular road. No, he smelt kind of...not like a wolf at all. Like he was hiding it.

That was impossible because only Omegas had that ability and only triggered wolves were Omegas. She tried again to access his thoughts. He had a barrier in place that she couldn't reach behind leaving only the surface emotions readable—Tad and Missy kissing passionately, naked bodies pressed close together, intense lovemaking that left them both covered in sweat—Missy broke the connection and bit back a moan of desire. What he wanted, she wanted.

By the time they pulled into the parking lot Missy was half out of her mind restraining herself from jumping Tad. She popped open her door and leapt into the blowing snow as soon as the truck shimmied to a stop.

Long deep breaths of icy cold air helped until Tad stepped around the cab with a concerned expression on his face.

"You okay, Missy?"

Oh, please don't look concerned. Concern was one step away from affection, and tonight her body could jump from affection to full sex with no trouble at all.

"I'm fine. Just needed some fresh air. Shall we go?" Missy forced herself to sound bright and cheerful. She hoped the place would be loud, dark and smoke-filled to dull her senses enough to get through the evening with Tad's virtue intact.

She wondered if he would appreciate the effort she was making. She had every intention of making love with him, but until she could visit the closest wolf pack and arrange for someone to tell Tad about his heritage she couldn't act.

Tad held the door open for her, and as she stepped past his arms, she knew she was done for. There was music, quiet and jazzy. The only smoke was from BBQ ribs. And the lighting was perfect to see Tad's eyes widen as he helped remove her coat.

"Fuck. Oops, sorry, but holy cow, you look good. I don't think I've ever..." Tad swallowed hard, his gaze tracing up the length of her legs to where her skirt ended high above her knees.

Fine. It wouldn't have met the *Catholic Girls School Uniform Requirements* but Missy was short and she need help to make her legs look longer. At least that was her excuse and she was sticking to it.

If she'd thought it through more she would have known this evening was going to be a bundle of dynamite waiting to detonate. Then she would have worn her baggy one-piece fleece hoodie that hung past her knees and a sloppy pair of sweat pants.

Liar.

She wouldn't have. She wanted Tad to drool over her. It made something deep inside very satisfied to see the admiration and the fire in his eyes.

She took a quick glance around. They would be safer sitting at the tall stools in front of the bar itself. Instead, Tad held her elbow and led her back toward a small booth tucked to one side of the bar. It was too late to protest, so she slid onto the soft leather upholstery behind the tiny table, her knees brushing Tad's as he followed her.

"What are you drinking tonight?" One of the servers stood waiting beside their table. Tad slipped his arm behind Missy, resting it along the back of the seat cushion, caressing her shoulders.

She was going to die. She really was. "Do they have—?"

"Sweetheart, first I'm gonna need to see some proof you're of legal age," the waitress interrupted.

Tad chortled as Missy dug into her purse cussing under her breath. She handed over her photo ID and poked Tad in the ribs to get him to stop. It really wasn't funny anymore.

The waitress handed it back with a wink. "Our bartender

can mix you any drink without looking it up. You name a drink he can't produce and it's on the house."

Missy glanced at the ceiling. She shouldn't do this. Not with needing to keep control over her body around Tad.

"What are you up to?" Tad teased with a squeeze to her shoulder.

Electrical lust shot through her and her mouth went dry. To hell with it. A challenge was a challenge and she could use a stiff drink. She smiled at the waitress.

"I'd like a Skip and Go Naked please."

Tad choked.

The waitress winked at her. "No problem, sweetheart. Tad, what'll it be for you tonight?"

"Rum and Coke, please."

The waitress left and Missy watched as she made her way back to the bar. She put in their orders and the bartender's head flicked in their direction. He lifted a hand and pointed at her, shaking his finger.

"What's a Skip and Go Naked, other than something that causes my heart to do double time?" Tad slipped his fingers over hers and Missy's mind drifted. She was supposed to concentrate on...something. Tad's beautiful brown eyes stared at her like she was the main dish at an all-you-can-eat dessert bar. Time slowed as she fell into the depths of his gaze. She leaned closer, his mouth inches away. If he'd ease a little more in her direction she be able to—

"You tried to trick me with that one." The bartender stood in front of them, a pale pink concoction in his hand. Missy made herself smile instead of baring her teeth at the man.

Her hormones were becoming a serious issue tonight.

"You thought if you missed the 'Hop' I wouldn't know it.

Hmmm? Well, you've got yourself one Skip and Go Naked. I left out the grenadine 'cause I figured that must be the hop."

Missy forced a laugh as she accepted the glass. "Actually, I've never heard of the Hop part. I'm glad you knew how to make one. It's been a long time. Thank you."

He kissed her hand and strutted back to his bar, king of all he surveyed. Missy took a short sip of the sweet drink before glancing at Tad. His eyes were dark, his face intense as he glared after the bartender. Missy frowned. "Tad? You okay?"

Tad shook his head like he was in a daze. "Sorry about that. I don't like how that fellow leers and touches everyone." He threw back half his drink and stood. "Come on, let's dance." He pulled her into his arms and Missy's vocal cords seized up. Tad folded her into him like a pillow into a slip. Every part of him nestled warm and smooth around her, solid and strong in all the right places. Warmth radiated from his core, and Missy concentrated on breathing in a slow, even rhythm. *Hyperventilating on the dance floor. Wonder if anyone ever called the ambulance for that one?*

Missy laid her head against Tad's chest and listened to his heartbeat. She was short enough that even with her high heels, his chin rested on top of her head, his arms reaching down to support her. She draped her hands around him, twining her fingers into the hair at his neckline. Tad hummed with pleasure.

As they swayed together to the bluesy music, Missy wondered if what she felt was possible. An untriggered male and a runaway Omega wolf, there was a strange combination. She closed her eyes and relaxed the tight reins she'd been keeping on herself. Tad dropped his hands and ran them over her back, down her hips, snuggling her tighter against his body, a rock-hard ridge pressing into her belly. The scent of his arousal wafted by on the air and she gasped back a groan. She wanted to taste so badly.

It was too much to continue to resist. Every nerve in her body screamed for him and she lost control. One flavour denied, she took the pleasure she could reach. Missy locked her fingers together, drew his mouth down and suckled his tongue. No gentle introduction, no soft finesse or enticement. Simple and hard desire drove her, his taste not even taking the edge off her need.

She slipped one leg on either side of his, pressed her heated core into his thigh with the thought that some release would be better than none. Tad seemed to read her mind. He feasted on her mouth like a starving man while he danced them into the shadows at the edge of the floor, away from any curious onlookers.

Tad dragged his lips from hers, his dark eyes snapping with need as he cupped her face in his hand. "You're playing with wildfire. Is this what you want? In public? Because we can go back to your hotel."

Missy gave a little jump and forced Tad to catch her. Going back to her room was out of the question. She couldn't—she wouldn't dare—have sex with Tad without him being aware of what his heritage was. She wasn't the one to tell him. But for tonight she was going to grasp the only thing she could and to hell with the consequences.

She wrapped her legs around him tighter, pressing against the solid ridge of his cock until he made an instinctive thrust at her. She let her head drop back, her hands clinging to his neck as he supported her hips in his hands. Somehow he shuffled them farther from the dance floor into a dusky little nook.

"More. Harder," Missy whispered. All her nerve endings flowed to one spot at the juncture of her thighs where he rubbed and thrust until the sensation of pleasure started to peak and a low sound escaped her lips. Tad covered her mouth with his hungry kisses as he increased the pounding against her, pressing her back into the wall behind them, each stroke caressing her clit like they were skin on skin.

The edge approached and she squeezed hard with her legs, adding the final bit of pressure she needed. She nipped at Tad's lip, breaking the skin and drawing blood that she sucked with a cry of pleasure. She melted from head to toe and let him catch her, her body uncontrollable as her orgasm rippled through her. Tad thrust another time or two, pressing as deep as the fabric between them would allow before he hissed and tensed as he came.

They stood wrapped in each other supported by the wall and a strange little ledge under her hips. His scent rose around them, thick and sweet on the air, and Missy's mouth watered. What they'd done was dangerous but the safest thing under the circumstances. She opened her eyes to see his chest heaving as he dragged air into his lungs.

She looked around curious where they ended up. It was an old phone nook. The privacy shield beside them was all that separated them from the front hallway and the line of people waiting to enter the bar. Missy tried to stifle her laughter, squirming in his arms. Tad opened his eyes, saw where they were and spun them to the right so they were both completely hidden.

He lowered her with gentleness to the phone shelf, hands tender as he adjusted her dress and smoothed her hair. He had such a sweet smile on his face she couldn't help running her hand over his cheek, stroking his jaw. Tad turned his face into her palm and kissed it. He winked at her.

"Thank you, AT&T."

Chapter Five

Tad tried to look casual and relaxed as he sat and waited for his sister to appear. Being around large groups of werewolves no longer freaked him out, but now he was in the midst of the Granite Lake pack elite. Beside him, Keil fidgeted with the medallion that was the symbol of his new position as they waited for Robyn.

Since Tuesday night and his date with Missy, it felt like Tad had worked twenty-hour days. The rest of the researchers had arrived and were in the process of establishing camp. Tad flew passengers and ferried supplies as quickly as possible but each day passed without time for more than a friendly public hello with Missy when he passed her at the camp where she slept.

The remaining hours he spent alternating between sleeping and taking cold showers.

He was going to force himself to relax tonight, try to forget big blue eyes, soft skin and passionate kisses, and celebrate his sister's wedding...wolf mating...whatever it was called.

Tad rotated the ice in his drink as he checked out the faces of the men sitting around him. There were no visible signs they could change into wolves, nothing to set them apart from the rest of society.

Other than, as Robyn put it, they were all freaking gorgeous.

While he'd been friends with these men for years, the stakes for the evening were much higher than flying a sightseeing party or back-country adventure group for Keil's guiding business. Tonight was invitation-only to celebrate Robyn's first shift to her wolf, and the acceptance of Keil and Robyn as the new Alphas for the Granite pack. Not only had Keil mated with Robyn, the two of them had shut down an attack on their lives and won the leadership of the pack.

He was never going to let his sister go anywhere alone ever again. Well, Keil would probably have something to say about it too, but *sheesh*. She was a danger to herself.

"She really made them shift?" Tad asked.

"Oh, not only that, she made them stand around and introduce themselves. Butt naked in the cold. Then they had to apologize to us both for 'disturbing the serenity of our honeymoon'. I thought Jack was going to pop a vein when she suggested he might like to look into purchasing some of the penis enhancers they advertise online."

Tad choked on his drink. "My sister?"

Keil exchanged knowing looks with his younger brother TJ. "Oh, yeah. She's amazing. Don't piss her off any more than you usually do. Now that she's wolf she's even more of a handful." Tad sat back and swallowed hard. Keil grinned at him. "Wait until she starts ordering you around."

All of a sudden Keil's sharp concentration on Tad blurred, his attention turning toward the door Robyn had disappeared behind. Soft scuffling noises came from the other side, and Tad realized Robyn and Keil were speaking to each other through their mate connection.

Another bloody amazing thing werewolves could do. One of the neatest as far as Tad was concerned, because Robyn had been deaf since she was four. She'd not only found her partner but she could hear again in a special way. Tad would still use sign language with her and she could read people's lips, but to hear someone speak again...

It must be amazing.

The door opened and Robyn stepped through, a pale blue robe draped over her shoulders. Her dark hair swung loose, and her eyes were bigger and brighter than Tad remembered.

His mouth fell open. He'd never seen Robyn look so gorgeous. She was his little sister, for heaven's sake, and he'd never thought of her as a girl before. As he watched her saunter toward Keil, it dawned on him she wasn't only a girl but a woman, and *the* woman to the highest-ranking wolf of this pack.

And she was head over heels in love. She and Keil both were. In fact it was damn uncomfortable to be in the same room watching the two of them. They looked like they'd forgotten others were present, and Tad thought some hot and heavy action would be starting in the next five seconds.

"Oh, gag." TJ rose from his chair and cut across the room pretending to slip his finger down his throat. He slid in front of Robyn and kissed her cheek before stepping back to ensure she could read his lips. "While I'm glad you're going to be my sister-in-law and my Alpha, can you save the sex for when you get in front of the pack?"

Tad choked again. *Holy crap.*

The colour drained from Robyn's face. She whipped around to glare at Keil. Tad's soon-to-be brother-in-law swallowed hard and shrugged. They were doing it again, he realized. Talking silently to each other.

Meanwhile TJ leaned over and patted Tad's shoulder kindly. "Don't worry, you can stop freaking out now. They'll be wolves. It's just one of those things," he whispered.

Tad shook his head in disbelief. "Yeah, well, excuse me if I still don't watch." He shivered. *Damn wolves and their openness about sex.*

Robyn flushed when Keil offered his arm, pausing for a second before shaking her head. She laid a hand on his elbow, and with a regal air they strolled through the door toward the main hall and the ceremony.

Tad loved to see the connection between them, see how much they cared for each other. If only he could find someone to complete him as well. Missy turned him inside out with sexual need and he loved being with her. The longing for more squeezed his throat shut. Could he really give up on the possibility of being able to shift into a wolf? He watched Robyn and Keil walk away, cuddled close and intimate, and his heart and mind fought to come to a decision.

Tad leaned against the wall in the shadows watching wolves and humans in various stages of undress wander the hall floor after the actual ceremony had finished. Seeing Robyn shift to wolf form for the first time had brought him to tears. He managed to wipe his eyes before anyone noticed and stood back to observe. Some of the pack removed their clothes and shifted to head outdoors with Robyn and Keil for a run. Others seemed content to visit at the tables lining the side of the hall.

Then it started.

"Well, what have we here? A half-blood lurking in the corner? Someone take out the trash for me."

Tad glanced down at an older woman, skin leathered by the sun. "Hey, I was—"

An overgrown ape pounded up to Tad and grabbed him by the arm. He gave Tad a brief sniff then choked. "Gag. Untriggered too. Move along, little puppy. This event is for big boys and girls. Invitation only." He began to drag Tad toward the exit doors.

"Hang on, I was invited—"

"Right. And I'm the Queen of Sheba." She tossed back her bleached hair. "It's riffraff like you that make me worry about bloodlines. Nasty thing."

Tad pulled hard and slipped away. He backed up quickly, darting a glance around the room to try to find a friendly face. A hand touched his shoulder and he acted on instinct and swung his fist landing a solid blow on...TJ's jaw.

Damn. That wasn't on the to-do list.

TJ flew backward to collapse at the feet of an angry crowd.

"See, just what I've said all along. We get no respect from half-bloods anymore." A skinny man pulled TJ to his feet and tried to brush him off. "I do hope you're all right, TJ. How extremely rude of this bum to hit you. Don't worry about him, we'll show him out."

TJ slapped the man's hands away and stomped up to Tad. Shaking his finger in Tad's face, TJ glared at him. "Do you know what you've done? Jerk. You cost me twenty bucks." He clapped Tad on both shoulders and his scowl turned to a grin. "I thought the brown-nosing would require at least a couple of hours to start. You've managed to get the suck-ups to show themselves not even fifteen minutes after Keil left the room. Good job, buddy."

TJ turned and stared back at the gathering crowd. "I suspected some of you were assholes, now I know for sure. Did any of you think to ask my friend who he was? You know, a visitor in town for a special occasion, let's welcome him, that kind of thing?"

The Queen of Sheba shoved to the front of the group and seemed intent on continuing to stir things up. "Why should we show him any manners? He's a half-blood. Untriggered. At his age that must mean he's packless."

"What's wrong, TJ?" The pack Beta, Erik, slipped beside them, his solid six-foot-five-inch frame an encouraging wall of safety.

TJ stared at the twenty or so wolves gathered in front of him. "Nothing's wrong. Tad and I were just reviewing Manners 101 with these morons. Let's go get something to eat while we wait for Keil and Robyn to return." He directed them toward the food, speaking over his shoulder. "I know Robyn will be happy to see *her brother* after she shifts back."

Stunned silence greeted his words.

"Oh come on, Tad, you knew wolves were just as bad as humans in some areas. Worse in others." Erik forced away another wolf who tried to pull up a chair and join them. "Ranking means only a little less than breathing to some of these jerks, and now that they know you're related to the Alpha—"

"—they all want to be my friend. I get it. I just don't like it. They didn't even want me in the building before. Is this an Alaskan thing? The Whitehorse pack had no problem accepting me as a half-blood. Untriggered. Heck, I don't know if it's a good idea for me to switch and join your pack, even if Robyn is now Alpha. Even if it's the closest pack to my work base." He shoved away his plate. He couldn't eat if he tried.

What had started as an amazing day had turned dark and cold.

"They're kissing up to you, are they?" Erik retrieved Tad's plate and pulled off an untouched chicken drumstick.

"I got accosted when I hit the can. The Queen of Sheba,

who must be close to eighty-five, offered me FirstMate." Tad shuddered. "I know I've been waiting a long time, but hell will freeze over before I accept her."

Erik grimaced. "Nasty. I hear you. Still, I'm sure there's someone else who's willing."

Tad shook his head. "Don't you see, what's the point? I don't want to have sex with someone who's willing because Robyn is Alpha. I want someone who wants me for, well, me. Is that too much to ask?"

"The issue is no one can sense how strong you are. The girls don't want to be trapped by a false mating," Erik pointed out. "And since you continue to turn down offers from mated females, you're out of luck."

"I still don't get why you don't want to just accept FirstMate," TJ complained. "The wolf offers, her mate is cool with it. Why aren't you? I mean, heck I know Keil would never allow it, but if Robyn *did* offer and he *did* agree and if *I* still had FirstMate to complete, which I don't, but if I *did* I would have no problem accepting a little loving from Miss Sweetcakes. Oww..." TJ howled as a firm grip on his ear twisted him to face Keil and Robyn, fully clothed and glaring daggers. TJ pulled a face.

Robyn lifted her arms and signed to Tad who hooted out loud. "Um, Robyn says it's Alpha Sweetcakes to you, TJ."

TJ grasped Keil's hand and attempted to rescue his ear. "My apologies, oh most high rulers, but you are one hot babe, Robyn. Just in case Keil ever forgets to tell you."

Robyn glanced back at Tad with a questioning look. He shook his head. There was no way he was explaining *that* conversation to her.

Tad pulled her in for a hug and a kiss, embracing her for a minute while he considered his options. Keil had asked him to stick around for a couple of days to help with sign language and make Robyn feel at home in Alaska with the Granite Lake pack. He'd originally said he'd do it, but now he knew it wouldn't work. Not if the last couple of hours were any indication. There was far too much politics involved, and while he liked to socialize and problem solve, there was no use in trying it here. His lack of official status would make it impossible for him to accomplish anything of value.

Tad stepped back and lifted his hands to talk to Robyn in American Sign Language, glad to have a way to enjoy a private conversation in the middle of the crowded room.

"You look amazing," he told her.

"I feel amazing. Oh, Tad, wait until you can shift. It's so..." She stopped and wrinkled her nose at him. "You don't feel comfortable here. You're leaving."

Tad dropped his hands in amazement. She really was a powerful wolf. "I see your damn Alpha insight is working already."

Robyn stuck her tongue out him briefly. "What's wrong?"

"I'm happy for you, sis. Really I am. In fact, this whole evening has helped me realize it's time to move on. I need to stop waiting for something to happen to make me satisfied and go *make* it happen."

Robyn frowned, her dark eyes staring into his. "Explain. You feel like you're a bubble ready to burst."

Tad sighed. It wasn't really time for this conversation, but it needed to be said. She deserved to know he'd finally arrived at a decision. "I don't want to mess up your celebration. It's just I'm not going to worry about trying to trigger my wolf anymore, okay? Keil explained to you it's tough for a half-blood like me to get triggered, and I've decided that I'm going to just ignore my wolf side and go make my human side happy instead."

A myriad of emotions flickered across Robyn face.

Confusion, disbelief, sadness. Then a hint of amusement. “What if you can have both? What you want as a human *and* what your wolf needs?”

Tad shook his head. “It’s not possible. You were lucky. You found Keil and you weren’t even looking for him. It’s better if I just forget the whole wolf thing.”

Robyn stomped her foot. “Bullshit. You can’t ignore your wolf and still be happy. That’s what was wrong with me before. I knew something was missing, and you will not believe how big a difference I feel now that my wolf is a complete part of me. Don’t give up. You really can be happy with yourself and trigger your wolf. I know it.”

“Making a proclamation as my Alpha?”

She rested her hands on her hips for a second, the gold flecks in her eyes swirling as she stared at him. Power rolled from her and his spine tingled. *Holy shit, she was strong.*

She raised her hands to sign again. “As both your Alpha and your sister. You’ve always looked out for me. I haven’t said thank you nearly enough. I love you, and I want you to be happy. It’s going to work out in the end.”

She punched him in the shoulder and pulled him in for another hug. She held on to both sides of his head and stared deep into his eyes for a moment. The wolf within her was beautiful to see, but he wasn’t the type to seize advantage of her good fortune. He wasn’t going to ride her coattails to get triggered. As much as the idea there was one special someone out there for him excited him, being with Missy was not a bad alternative. Partners for life was what he wanted, even if it meant his wolf remained trapped.

“Tad, hang on.” Erik placed a restraining hand on Tad’s

door. “Keil needs to talk to you before you go.”

Tad was tired, fed up and ready to go home to collapse and dream about Missy. “Can it wait?”

Erik froze. He turned and raised a brow at Tad.

“Oh shit. Sorry.” *Damn, damn, damn.* He really needed to remember who he was talking to at times. The whole werewolf code was like some kind of mystical Ten Commandments, and Tad seemed to constantly break the rules, one way or another. He relocked his door and fell into step with the giant man.

Erik spoke softly. “You can get away with a lot, being related to Robyn and all, but it’s not a good idea—”

“I know, I know, the whole ‘Alpha is King’ thing. I have trouble remembering at times. It doesn’t seem real, maybe because I can’t shift. I guess I’m not a very good wolf.” Tad had to walk double-quick to keep up with the strides of his new Beta.

“How can you not remember?” Erik asked. “Don’t you feel like you’ve got to listen when Keil talks? Or your previous Alpha in Whitehorse?”

Tad shrugged. “I guess. Well, sometimes. Sometimes I just feel annoyed.”

“Annoyed?” Erik sounded strange, like he had swallowed something the wrong way.

Tad flicked a glance up at him. “Annoyed or even pissed off. Usually when I think it’s a thing stupid for them to ask. I don’t think Keil’s ordered me to do anything yet, so I’m not sure, but my Alpha in Whitehorse, heck, I ignored him all the time.”

Erik was no longer at his side and Tad turned back to look at the man who was several paces behind making the weirdest face. This night was turning truly bizarre.

“What?” Tad watched as the Beta walked a slow circle around him, sniffing the air. “Sod off—I hate it when people do that." Tad forced him away. Not an easy task since Erik was built like a brick shithouse with reinforced metal corners.

Erik shook his head slowly. "Keil's gonna blow a gasket."

"Tad's going to pitch a fit if he doesn't get to go home soon. Stop with the wolfy mumbo jumbo and let's go see the Big Cheese." Tad stormed into the hall, Erik trailing behind him chuckling.

Keil met them at the front foyer and motioned for his Beta to stand watch.

"You're making me nervous. Is something wrong?" Tad asked, glancing around the empty space. He didn't see any trouble but something was odd about the way Keil looked at him.

Keil put a reassuring hand on his shoulder and led them to some overstuffed chairs at the side of the area. "No, you're fine, Robyn's fine, all that kind of stuff. I need to talk to you about something serious before you leave."

Tad waited.

"It's kind of a delicate subject with you, and I didn't think I should mention it in front of the others."

Tad waited.

Keil rolled his eyes. "You're not going to make this easy on me, are you?"

Tad grinned at the big man. It was the most entertainment he'd had all night. Then his smile faded as he got an inkling of the topic at hand. "Oh crap, you're not going to tell me someone's offered me FirstMate, are you?"

Keil frowned. "I thought you'd be pleased. You've been waiting forever—"

Tad's blood started to boil. Enough was enough. "Keil, I don't want to fuck someone who's brown-nosing for you. Forget it."

"She's not trying to impress me."

"Yeah. Right. Let me guess. Is she a skinny blonde with a tan?"

Keil sat back. "Well, I wouldn't call her skinny, but she is blonde. You know who offered?"

Tad pulled a sour expression. "She offered herself to me already and I thought I would lose my dinner. You don't really think I should accept her, do you? I know it's not forever but I do have to look at her for a couple days. And touch her..." He shivered. The thought of being intimate with the Queen of Sheba turned his stomach. "Thanks, but no thanks."

Anger flared across Keil's face. "If this is how picky you are, no wonder you've never been triggered. I thought we finally found a solution you'd be pleased with." Keil picked up one of the cushions from the couch and smacked it with his fist. He raised his dark eyes to glare at Tad.

He glared back until he remembered this was both his new Alpha and his new brother-in-law. Tad sighed and lowered his gaze. "I don't think I'm being picky."

"Who are you waiting for, Miss Wolf Canada?" Keil demanded.

Tad gaped at him. *No way.* "Is there such a thing?"

"Arghhh!" Keil threw the pillow at him.

Tad held up his hands, trying to calm Keil down. "Look, I'm not trying to be difficult."

"Well, you're managing to piss me off and you're going to get me in shit with my mate. Robyn was so excited at the possibility you'd get triggered soon."

Like that was going to change Tad's mind about the whole thing. "I'm not fucking someone for Robyn's sake."

"It's just FirstMate. Get over it."

Tad shook his head.

Keil crossed his arms over his chest. "Then *you* get to explain yourself to Robyn because she thought you'd be thrilled. She said Missy was one of the—"

"What?" Tad leapt forward in his seat. *Who did Keil say?* "Wait a second, rewind. Who are we talking about here? Did you say Missy?"

"Damn right. Gorgeous woman like that offers you—"

"She's a wolf?" Holy crap, Missy offered FirstMate? Sweet, beautiful, sexy-as-all-get-out Missy who turned him inside out with longing? His heart pounded harder and suddenly it was difficult to breath.

Keil pinched the bridge of his nose. "Shit, are you never going to learn how to pick up a scent? Yes, Missy is a wolf. She came by yesterday to tell me she was in the area. As the nearest pack, it's a courtesy thing to check in. She caught the whole hullabaloo about me and Robyn taking over leadership, and you not being triggered, and she said she'd be delighted to offer you FirstMate. Seems she's had a soft spot for you since high school. Since you aren't interested and the mere thought of touching her causes your face to turn green I guess I should just—"

"Will you slow down?" Tad hopped from his chair and began to pace. His nerves jangled for a second then relaxed as a faint trail of hope began to build. But why had Missy not mentioned anything? "I didn't know she was a wolf. We went on a date the other day and she never said a word to me."

"She wasn't sure you knew about your wolf genes until she met Robyn." Keil looked puzzled. "Just who did you think I was suggesting?"

Missy wanted to have sex with him. Tad fought down the

images that flared in his mind to concentrate on answering Keil. "I thought you were talking about the chick with the shimmery pink highlights in her hair."

Keil laughed and shook his head. "Okay, now your reaction makes sense. So now that we're talking the same language, what do you think? Missy's a widow, so your little issue about not doing the deed with a married woman is a moot point. Plus she's excessively easy on the eyes. Not that I would notice, being totally enamored by your sister and all."

Tad snorted. "I think the expression is 'married, not dead'. Missy is flipping gorgeous and you know it. Robyn would say the same."

"So..."

"Man, this still seems so forced and weird. Like a prearranged trip to the local brothel." He'd learned to be a lot more open about discussing sex over the past two years, but the upfront and in-your-face wolf method still made him squirm. Fine, he and Missy would do FirstMate. Now he didn't want to talk about it anymore.

Keil smirked. "I think you can get over that little problem. From what Missy told me you seemed interested enough in her the other day, so get together and—"

"Shit, she told you what we did?" *And was Robyn in the room to hear it?* That's all he needed, his sister knowing he was a sex fiend.

Damn, Robyn already knew Missy had offered. That was the point of her whole mysterious conversation about getting what both his human and wolf sides wanted. He couldn't stop the heat that rose to his face.

"No, but you've got me curious. You want to tell me what you did that's got you going from zero-to-sixty in three seconds flat? I've never seen a guy react like that before."

"Shut up, Keil." His new brother-in-law's hearty laugh rang out and Tad gave him a sheepish grin. "Yeah, I'm interested. Only, let me set the pace, please. I'll be working with her for the next while, and I don't think it's good if we hit the sack and have at it." As much as he'd like to.

Holy smoke, Missy was a wolf. She'd offered FirstMate. They were going to have sex. He'd been waiting for years to find someone to trigger him, and now it wasn't only going to happen, it was going to happen with Missy.

Wow. High school dreams could come true.

Chapter Six

Tad made a final check of the aircraft instruments and tucked away the flight plan and weather reports. There were only eight hours of daylight to play with and they needed to head out soon.

The meteorologist, Missy's working partner in the project, detained them. Tad had flown the man for hours the day before and discovered Dan was anal when it came to details. Today he not only fussed with last-minute changes, he wasn't feeling well, disappearing every ten minutes on a bathroom run.

"Missy, can we get started and at least put the first of the relays into place?" Tad suggested, chomping at the bit to get moving. "Then we can contact Dan and let him do his thing with the base unit at camp. It's going to require at least twenty minutes to get to the first drop spot before you can even turn anything on to start linking the receivers."

It was the first time he'd seen Missy since he and Keil spoke on Saturday. She looked breathtaking as usual, but he imagined there was a little something extra in her smile when she responded to him. Heat flared between them, and he forced himself to turn away before he did something too wolfish—like pounce on her in public.

By the time they were in the air wearing headsets so they could communicate, he thought he'd worked out what he wanted to say. It needed to be something tender and sweet, yet let her know he was interested in her not only for FirstMate reasons but because he really liked her as a person. It wasn't just about sex, even though she was hot enough to cause spring thaw to set in early—

"Tad?" Missy's smooth voice came through the speakers fuzzy with static. His cock still stood up and paid attention.

"Yes?"

"When we're done today would you like me to come back to your apartment or do you want to get a hotel room? Because all my stuff is at the camp and I don't think we should have sex there."

It took a couple of seconds for Tad to level the plane. Blunt-speaking wolves. Got him every time.

"I brought along a change of clothes in my duffle bag so we can go straight to wherever you want."

"Missy!" Tad adjusted his pants to regain a little blood flow.

She snickered and he turned a sheepish smile in her direction. Her eyes sparkled with desire as she held out her hand and he clasped it, his thumb rubbing across her knuckles in a gentle caress.

So soft. So right.

A faint hint of her scent surprised him, either perfume or her natural fragrance, as it filled his nostrils and sent his body into overdrive. Tad scrambled through some quick calculations while there was still blood in his brain. Twelve relays to set up at fifteen minutes each. Adding flight time, landing and storage for the plane, driving and sprinting up the stairs, they could be at his place by two p.m. at the latest.

All ready for some Afternoon Delight.

✧

"I *did* change the frequency over, Dan." Missy held her head in one hand while she spoke into the radio. "If you're not receiving the feedback you missed something at your end."

Tad paced behind her in the snow, his collar turned up against the icy wind. It was after three and there was often a breeze on the glacier by this time of day. Another reason he'd hoped to be safe at home before now.

"I know it's not a problem on my end... No, I won't turn it off and recalibrate because that would require another twenty minutes and it wouldn't fix the problem... Dan?" Missy dropped the phone. "He's throwing up again. I don't believe this!"

Over the day Dan had turned a simple exercise into a new form of hell. Of course, Tad was a trifle biased since he had hoped to be strolling through paradise right about now. The other man fumbled and upset every weather relay Missy tried to arrange. Between running a fever and running to the bathroom, he had helped link together only seven of the twenty needed relays.

It would be dark in a short time and Tad dreaded the idea of spending the night on the glacier in his plane. "Missy, we've got to stop. Tell whomever you can reach we're coming in. Dan's too sick to finish and we're heading into the danger zone."

Missy nodded and relayed the message to base camp. Their response made her eyes grow wide with concern. As she tucked away the phone and gathered her things, passing Tad the extra packages to store back in the cargo hold, she shared the news. "We can't do any more today anyway. They've returned Dan to his tent. He's unconscious."

Back on board Tad examined the flight line. The wind direction had changed enough that the new direction for takeoff wasn't going to be pleasant. "Umm, you might like to close your eyes. The plane will be a little tight to the trees before we get airborne."

Missy nodded and put on her headset. "I trust you."

Tad swallowed. Holy crap, now his chest was as tight as his throat. The way Missy put herself into his hands so quickly and faithfully was humbling.

He made it off the glacier with inches to spare. The relentless wind swept ice particles over the body of his plane like harsh sandpaper. Both hands fought to control the little craft and all was going well until a series of bright orange warning lights flashed on the instrument panel. The foul weather was screwing with the wing flaps.

Oh. Shit.

Even worse was the red engine light that blazed a second later.

The sun was sinking, frightening yet beautiful, through the haze of the blowing snow. Tad knew where he was. He'd double and triple checked his maps while he'd waited for Missy to finish each relay.

They weren't going to make it back to Haines Junction in this weather with the plane in trouble. They might be able to make it to Keil's mountain retreat—with a little luck. He glanced at Missy, who watched him with confidence.

Hell, forget the luck. For her, he'd pull off a miracle.

✧

Tad guided Missy through the deep snow toward the cabin as the wind howled around them.

"Will we have to break in?" She had to shout to be heard.

"Nope. I know the secret code. I've flown Keil and his clients here many times, and they shared their tricks." He pulled them past the front door to the large side window where a combination lock hung on the hasp. "Four-letter combo. TJ set it, I bet." He dialed in H-E-L-P and pulled.

Nothing.

Tad tried O-P-E-N, then S-A-V-E. He cursed into the wind.

"What should it be set for?" Missy asked, tucked in tight against his side. She tried to contain her shivers. The temperature was dropping fast and her teeth chattered. As glad as she was that Tad had landed them safely, it was far colder than she was used to. She was tempted to shift to her wolf and curl up in a ball to get warm.

"Keil uses the three-tumbler lock and sets it to SOS or nine-one-one for emergencies. TJ likes to use the four-tumbler lock and he tends to get fancy. What would you say if you needed to get in the cabin and had no key?"

"I'd probably swear." She stuck her hands farther into her armpits and hopped on the spot.

Tad gave her cheek a quick you're-a-genius kiss and warmth shot through her. He had the lock off in a moment, the window open, and he lifted her in. Tad crawled through behind her and pulled the window shut. The relative silence echoed in her ears.

"What was the word?"

Tad directed her toward the airtight stove. "S-H-I-T. That boy needs to grow up." He grabbed a blanket out of a sealed Rubbermaid tote and wrapped it around her shoulders. He stared at her for a second, his cold fingers soft against her cheek before he covered her more thoroughly. "Sit here and I'll get the fire started. We'll have everything we need in a minute. Keil is nothing if not prepared."

Missy watched, huddled under the blanket, as Tad lit the stove and hustled around the kitchen area pulling things from inside sealed boxes. Tea, sugar, canned spaghetti sauce and dry pasta all appeared on the sideboard. By the time the stove radiated heat into the main space of the cabin, there was melted snow for boiling the pasta and the rich aroma of tomato sauce filled the air.

Such smooth movements for an untriggered wolf. There was a kind of innate grace in most shifters, a carryover from their wolf form. Tad had yet to turn into his wolf, but Missy could imagine him. She bet he would be pale silver, as light as she was, even though his human form was dark in skin and hair. He was going to be beautiful. Just like his human.

As she watched her desire for him grew. Her body tightened and moisture began to gather in her core. This day had been a long time coming and her skin tingled in anticipation of his touch. Missy was glad that she would get to share this experience with him. No matter how dangerous it was for her to offer him FirstMate. With all she'd been through in the Whistler pack, the years of being unloved and trapped in a marriage of convenience, she needed to do one last special thing for herself. Whatever the result.

She was grateful to have something special she could give to Tad.

She got up to change out of her wet things into the clothes she'd brought along. Tad watched her open her bag without saying anything, his gaze hot as she reached in and pulled out a thick pair of pants.

"Sweats. Hmm, baby, you're my kind of woman," Tad teased, his smile brightening the room.

"It's cold here after living away from the north," Missy complained.

Tad winked at her. "What else you got in that bag of tricks?

Here I thought you meant you'd brought a sexy nightie or massage oil."

Missy pulled out a thick pair of wool socks and her hairbrush.

"Ropes and a paddle, right?"

Missy blew a raspberry at him and ducked behind the stack of boxes while Tad turned back to the stove, but not before they both cast a final glance at each other. The sexual intent in Tad's gaze burned her and she had to take a long, slow breath before she could change.

Warm food filled their bellies and the heat from the stove reached even the farthest corners of the cabin. Missy sighed and leaned back on the soft pillows Tad had pulled from storage and placed in front of the fire.

"There were three other full-blood wolves in high school with us," she said, watching the expressions on his face with delight. "Do you know who they were?"

Tad propped himself on his elbows beside her. "I know about Leon. He still belongs to the pack in Whitehorse. I suspected there was something different about him even before I knew about wolves."

Missy laughed. "Why?"

Tad bunched his shoulders and screwed his face into a grimace. He deepened his voice and rasped out, "'Cause if you'd ever seen the guy changing for gym class you'd have thought he'd forgotten to complete a shift. Guy needs shares in Nair."

She giggled. That was Leon to a T. "You're bad. Who else?"

"I'm not sure. Cindy moved away shortly after you did. She had the whole 'look but don't touch' thing down to perfection and you two hung out together a lot around school and in town…" He paused.

"You were watching me, weren't you?" Missy said with her gaze on his lips, on the corner of his mouth. Her tongue slipped out to wet her own lips, unable to stop the automatic gesture.

"All the time," Tad admitted quietly. He reached out a hand and tugged loose a curl. She swallowed hard as his touch sent a riot of sensation through her body. "You fascinated me. You still do."

He continued to stare at her, his eyes growing darker.

"I need to kiss you." His voice was harsh and low as he continued to twirl her hair around his finger. "I really need to kiss you now."

He didn't come closer. What was he waiting for? Missy licked her lips again and he groaned as his hand cupped her neck to pull her in. They were a mere whisper apart. His breath warmed her, and still he didn't move closer and touch her. Then she realized he wouldn't. He waited for her. It was her call, her decision.

"Missy?" His voice teased her skin, tickled her senses, drew the very air from her lungs.

She dropped her mouth the final quarter inch and their lips touched, tentative, hesitant. Tad cradled her close, his hands tender as he massaged her neck and shoulders, his lips soft and restrained.

What she wanted was more. She stroked her tongue over his mouth, teased at the seam of his lips and urged him to open. With a groan he complied, and she snuck inside to lick his teeth. Heat rose around them as Tad joined her, his tongue sweeping hers as he dragged their bodies into contact, hips together, her torso tight to his chest.

The cozy blankets under them, the warmth of the fire filling the room, the crackle as the logs settled, all these sensations faded away as his physical touch overwhelmed her. His hands slipped under her sweatshirt and glided down her back. Their bodies pressed together. Her nipples, tight and hard, rubbed against him.

Through it all they kissed. The intoxicating touch of mouth on mouth thrilled her, made her lightheaded. She pulled away an inch to gasp in air, and found she looked up at Tad. He'd rolled them over without her even being aware of it. He watched her carefully as he held his full weight on his forearms, suspending himself above her body. His hardness nestled against her thigh.

His laboured breathing showed her she wasn't the only one affected.

She stared at him. "You kiss better than a dream."

Tad's eyes widened. "Sweetheart, do you have any idea how many dreams you've starred in for me?"

He continued to gaze at her and Missy flushed. Her hands were locked around his neck, his hair standing straight up from where she'd clutched at him while they kissed. "I, umm... What was the question?"

Dark eyes flashed at her. "No questions. Just more of this."

He lowered his head and she was gone, lost in his taste, his touch. He nuzzled at her neck, teeth rasping her skin, and her womb clenched. Moisture, hot and slick, flooded from her body. Blood rushed to her pussy lips until they were swollen and aching.

Tad shifted to the side and his hand passed over her belly to cup her breast. He drew in sharp breath.

"Shit, Missy. You're not wearing a bra."

She thrust her chest into firmer contact with his hand. Electric shocks slid through her as he nestled the globe of her breast in his palm, his thumb brushing her nipple with a ghostly touch.

Muttered words of passion reached her ears. He pushed up her sweater with his hand and lapped at the taut peak. Covering the whole areola, he suckled hard. A line flared from his mouth to her core, lightning flashed and she cried out as she clutched him tight.

She'd never felt anything like this before. She needed him, needed his desire, his mouth. She was empty and only Tad could fill her. He switched to her other breast, slipping his hand back past her belly to the waistband of her sweats. As he slid his fingers under the elastic, she opened her legs in welcome, tugging on his hair to force his head to her mouth. His taste was addictive and she wanted more.

As Tad's fingers brushed her mound he drew another quick breath then spoke against her lips. "Girl, you're killing me. No bra, no panties... Oh damn, you're wet."

His hand cupped her mound, one finger slid through her curls to part her sensitive lips. His finger nestled just inside her sheath.

Missy closed her eyes and drank in the sensations as a shiver raced over her skin. His lips, demanding a response, feasted on her mouth, yet the hand that explored her pussy was soft. He stroked her, slow and controlled, even as he kissed her hard and furious. His body shook and she wondered how much longer he would last.

She didn't want gentle anymore. The desire to be filled, to be seized by Tad and completely possessed, overwhelmed her. His scent hung strong in the air, filling her nose, her mouth.

Her heart.

Her soul.

Tendrils of emotion passed briefly between them and her

eyes flew open with surprise. Oh, sweet mercy, it really was happening. The mate connection. She'd been told what to expect but never thought she would experience it. She closed her eyes and tried to calm herself. Being tied to Tad with a false mating meant she would escape from her Alpha's clutches and that had been the goal. But she'd never expected the connection to feel so real.

She must have made a small sound not in keeping with their lovemaking because Tad pulled back. He dropped his forehead to her shoulder and took a few deep breaths. He shifted to pull away, but she caught at his shoulders, wrapping a leg around him to freeze him in position.

"I wasn't telling you to stop. You're the best lover I've ever—"

"Let's not talk about other people loving you," Tad gritted through his teeth. He rolled to the side, keeping their legs in contact. "For some reason the thought makes me want to shoot someone."

Missy stared at him. Was it possible? She knew what she felt. The emotional desire to be with him was even stronger than the physical compulsion. And the physical was off the charts. She cupped his face in her hands and reached out with her Omega sense into his mind, into the emotions and needs hidden away. Images flashed—naked bodies twined together, children playing in a field, two hands clasped that were wrinkled with time—Missy gasped.

She'd been wrong all along. She'd assumed her desire for him was a false reading when really she should have known.

He *was* her mate. Her real, honest-to-goodness, forever-and-always mate.

"Oh, Tad." This was more overwhelming than she'd ever imagined it could be. With his taste rioting through her body and the images from his mind encouraging her, it was all she could do to stop from stripping off their clothes and jumping his bones.

Not that it was a bad idea.

She trembled in his arms and Tad came close to losing control. He looked into her eyes, checking to see if she was afraid. *Fuck.* He must have done something, moved too fast, not shown how much she meant to him. Pain, deep and sharp, thrust into him and he sucked in a breath.

"Sweetheart, what's wrong?" Tad tried to untangle their limbs, he tried, but his body wouldn't cooperate. Leaving the heat of her touch would wrench his heart from his body.

"Nothing's wrong, everything's right." She cupped his face in her hands again, the softness of her touch washing over him with equal parts of desire and peace. There was something so right about Missy, so far beyond mere sex that his mind grew foggy and it was hard to concentrate on her words. "Can you feel it? This isn't just FirstMate, it's more. You and I, we're mates."

Tad froze. It wasn't possible. She'd had a mate, yet for some reason she was getting the message they belonged together forever. Oh bloody hell, it was the frickin' werewolf hormones again. Somehow she was getting a false positive.

How could this happen? How could it happen without them having sex? She was going to think she was in love with him for the rest of her life and it would just be pheromones controlling her. He couldn't do that, couldn't treat someone he cared about in such a cold, heartless manner, especially Missy. Tad summoned strength he didn't know he had from within and dragged himself away.

They both cried with low moans as he stumbled across the room to put distance between them. The physical pain that shot through his body was unexpected and nearly drove him to his knees. His eyes blurred for a moment and the room spun as he grew light-headed.

"I'm so sorry, I really am." He would do anything to stop from hurting her. His limbs shook as he leaned on the doorframe. His body was on fire, even more than when he was touching her.

She was pale, confusion written all over her face, and he ached for her. The situation was beyond her control and entirely his fault. "I thought, I mean..." She hesitated before closing her tear-filled eyes and starting to shake. "Don't you want me?"

A sound of agony ripped from his throat at the thought of denying his need for her. Bloody werewolf genes had messed up his life and now Missy's. All he wanted was to hold her and make it all better, but it wasn't possible. Everything he'd been told over the years meant she had to be mistaken and unless he stopped now she would suffer forever. He softened his voice and let his caring come through as he spoke. "Hell, it's not you, it's me. Don't you see? I'm not triggered. We can't be mates, it's the pheromones blinding you. You just think I'm your mate. Oh, sweetheart, I wish it was true." He wished it with everything he had.

"It is!" Missy cried. She was on her knees now, her sweater askew, hair tousled everywhere.

He'd never seen anything as beautiful. It was sheer torture to drop his gaze from her, his heart pounding fast, his ears ringing as blood roared through his head. He forced down his lust to try and reason with her. "I can't be. You have a mate." It never happened twice. A once-in-a-lifetime event and when they died, a piece of you died.

"I had a husband, Tad. Not a mate. We were married but it was a political thing forced upon me." She rose and reached for him.

Tad held out a hand to stop her, his mind spinning. She'd never had a mate. She'd said *they* were mates. Could she be right? He sniffed hard. The only aroma that reached him was the faint scent of wood smoke. His sinus passages were plugged, his forehead felt hot. His body ached.

Did he want her? Hell yeah, but there didn't seem to be the irresistible connection that he'd been warned occurred when true mates met. He wanted to bury himself in her and protect her, but he'd felt that way since they were kids back in high school. The connection, the pull, he felt equally strongly with his human side. How could this possibly be a true mating if he wasn't sure? The trickle of doubt that remained tied his hands.

Tied his heart.

Then for one evil, wicked moment Tad was tempted to continue. To take her and make love to her so she'd be trapped forever. He loved her, damn it. She would love him. Did it matter that it would just be chemicals on her side? His human morals fought a battle of epic proportions against the desires of the wolf raging through him. The lust, the need to be triggered.

A cooling breeze flowed around him and in that brief second his heart broke. He'd nearly done the one thing he'd sworn he'd never do, take advantage of someone he cared about.

He couldn't. She had to be set free. All his dreams fell to the ground and shattered. The need that had risen in his body overflowed to his mind and drawing back from her was the hardest thing he'd ever done. The room blurred again. It was impossible to think straight.

"If you were never mated that means there's no chance we could ever safely share FirstMate. I can't do that to you. I can't risk making you suffer thinking you're in love with me for the rest of your life." His tongue tripped over the words, awkward, painful. He wanted her but he wanted the best for her more.

"But, Tad—"

"Missy, hush." Tad dropped his voice, calmed his pounding heart. He had to explain he wasn't rejecting her but saving her from a grave mistake. "Falling in love with someone for real and thinking you're in love because your damn werewolf hormones are controlling you aren't the same thing. Somewhere out there you have a real mate with whom you'll connect intimately. If I take advantage of you, I'd be destroying the future you could have. The absolute joy. The complete belonging. I care too much for you to let you give up on all that. We have to stop, now." Tad snatched up his coat and shoved his feet into his boots haphazardly, the room spinning as he moved. "Keep the fire going. I'll be back later. Don't leave the cabin. I'm going to try the radio again."

"Tad, don't leave me, I ache… It hurts. Don't leave—"

He closed the door on the sound of her quivering voice and dropped his shoulder back to seal it shut. Sharp knives cut through his limbs, his throat was raw and his heart was a block of ice within his chest. He stumbled down the stairs and back toward the plane. There had to be a way to get out of here soon.

Before he died from the pain of a broken heart.

Chapter Seven

Missy fell to her knees, a cry tearing from her lips. How could he leave after being told they were mates? *Damn overly considerate asshole.* Every cell in her body screamed at her to follow, to drag him back into the cabin and force him to finish what they'd started.

She dropped her head to the floor and concentrated. Her skills as an Omega calmed her so she could think, could function until Tad regained his senses and returned. Long, slow breaths helped relieve the hardest edge of her pain as she stretched the hormone-tightened muscles of her arms and legs. After what seemed to be hours, Missy crawled to the table and pulled herself up.

Stumbling to the door, she forced her legs to cooperate as she drove herself to keep moving. Part of her body wanted to shut down and retreat under the blankets to shake until Tad came back and eased her pain. But if what she'd guessed about him was right, Tad wasn't aware of all the physical rules for wolves. He might not want to mate with her, but he had little choice in the matter now. The chemical switch had begun to flip and they needed each other to survive.

"Just saying no" wouldn't be enough.

She tugged the door open and stared into whiteout conditions. The wind shook the roof of the cabin. It was hard to see the stairs five feet away at the edge of the covered porch as the snow streaked across in sheets.

If Tad was anywhere but in the airplane he was in danger.

She pulled off her clothes, her teeth chattering from more than being cold. Her skin was so sensitive each touch of her own hands tore her body apart with pain. Tad could be as considerate as he wanted some other time. Right now she was going to haul his ass back and force him to take her.

Missy stepped onto the porch naked, skin lashed by ice particles that stung like wasps. She lowered herself to the ground and shifted, the comfort of the change to wolf easing part of the pain even as missing her mate hurt at a deeper core level.

She felt him out in the storm. Tad had tried to deny they were mates, but there was no way to deny the connection. It was like a string tied between them that she could easily follow.

She leapt off the porch and listened for a moment, the harsh cry of the wind different to her lupine ears. Little creatures huddled under the porch, their tiny bodies hiding from the winter's fury. Larger animals roamed in the more protected trees, including at least one natural wolf. He would know she was there. He would know she was one of his kind and yet not his kind, and he'd be wary. She let a little of her Omega awareness slip away to reassure him before she turned to track her mate.

The wind had already obliterated a large part of Tad's footprints, the holes filled with the driven snow. The trail she followed wandered as Tad had staggered on unsteady feet. How he managed to flee so far from her showed incredible strength.

Or stubbornness that bordered on the moronic.

She approached the plane, fear rising within her. She sensed Tad's heartbeat slowing, not through meditation, but because he was in danger. Ahead by the ski of the plane, there was a snow-covered mound. She raced up to discover him crumpled face down on the ground. She threw back her head and howled, a long high cry of command, before she stuck her muzzle to the side of his face and sniffed.

The initial hit of his scent raced through her with the impact of shooting a mickey of tequila. Her head spun, her mouth watered and the sexual tension throughout her body flared again just being in his presence. But she also felt the danger. Tad was burning up. His body shook with fever, and even if she woke him, she'd never be able to carry him. She cried out again, louder this time, more demanding.

Missy used her paws and her teeth to drag Tad closer to the plane and the slight protection of the hillside before she curled around his head, her warm breath on his face. She watched for any sign of movement, in Tad or in the whitened air beyond them.

"Missy?" Tad's voice was a soft rasp.

She licked his neck.

"I'm sorry, Missy. I'm so sorry."

Missy's head flicked to attention.

They came. The natural wolves crept up to where Tad lay, the leader's eyes on Missy. She stared him down, not moving from her protective position around Tad. Slowly the timber wolf approached and lowered himself to the ground by her paws. He lapped at her mouth for a moment and she gave him a nudge with her head.

They would be all right.

A few minutes later Missy double-checked the pile of furry bodies that covered Tad to keep him warm until she returned with help. She nudged the leader of the group in farewell then turned away.

✧

Pain stroked the back of his neck, wrapped gently around his forehead and then socked him between the eyes. Tad would have groaned but that required too much energy. Panting seemed the limit of his ability to complain at the moment.

"So, zombie boy. You gonna get your ass out of bed sometime this week or what?" His partner's loud voice echoed like he was using a megaphone.

"You think he's going to remember anything this time, Shaun?"

"Don't know, TJ. I think it's pretty amusing myself. How about we tell him he's been booked to fly the Queen on her next royal tour?"

They were talking nearby but Tad couldn't see them. "Hey, guys. Shut up for a minute. Which one of you dropped the anvil on my head?"

"Hmm, good sign. He's being an asshole," Shaun said.

"Why can't I see you?" Tad thought his eyes were open but it was so dark in the room he couldn't be sure.

A faint shimmer of light came through as Shaun cracked open the curtains. "It's nighttime and we've got your summer light-blocking curtains closed. The pack doctor said with the fever you needed it as dark as possible to avoid complications." He paced over and sat, the most concerned look on his face Tad had ever seen. "How do you feel?"

Tad tried a slow stretch. He had aches on tops of aches, his head pounded and there was something he needed to remember. "Did I catch the flu or something?"

Tad watched TJ and Shaun exchange glances. "Yeah, or

something. Remember that guy you flew around for hours? He came down with a bad case of the nasties, and since you had the pleasure of his company in close quarters, you were a nice little time bomb waiting to happen," Shaun explained.

TJ snorted. "Of course racing into a freaking blizzard didn't help matters. The only reason you survived is—"

"TJ, go make some coffee. Thanks." Shaun turned his back on TJ in dismissal.

Tad attempted a laugh as TJ left the room. "How did you do that? I thought no one could get TJ to shut up when he gets started."

Shaun reached for Tad's forehead. "It's a wolf thing. I rank higher and I only use the authority when it's needed." In slow motion Shaun touched his skin.

Giant invisible ice picks appeared and starting jabbing him everywhere. He jerked away from Shaun's hand, swearing under his breath. His head spun and his skin crawled. "What the hell is that about?"

"You really want to know?"

Tad threw a pillow at Shaun. "What kind of stupid-ass remark is that? Of course I want to know. My head is throbbing and I feel like I've been tied to an ant hill after being dipped in honey."

"Ooooh. Nice analogy, flyboy. You remember where you got the honey from?"

Tad got ready to yell at Shaun to tell him to start making sense and then... "Oh shit, is Missy all right?"

Shaun clapped his hands together with exaggerated enthusiasm. "Finally, the right question. You *are* on the cutting edge of sanity this time. Yes, Missy is as good as can be expected."

"What's that mean? And why are you acting so weird?" Tad

threw back the covers and swung his legs to the floor, intending to get dressed. The room had other ideas as it spun in a one-eighty, and the roof flipped to the floor. Tad found himself flat on his back, this time on the carpet.

"Let's try this again. How are you feeling, Tad?"

Nothing was working right and his brain felt like it was iced up. "Good grief, what's wrong with me?"

Shaun's voice grew quiet with an annoying "I'm being patient" undertone. "You've been sick, Tad. You caught the flu from the guy you flew around—"

Fuck that. "Yeah, you told me." Tad held a hand out to Shaun to get a pull upright. Shaun hid his arms behind him and Tad cursed. He rolled to his belly and gave a painful push onto his knees.

"Not that I don't want to help but listening to you scream in pain every time someone touches you lost its appeal after the first dozen times." Shaun sat on the chair next to the bed.

Tad crawled back onto the mattress and covered himself. The pressure of the quilt on his skin hurt less than the cold seeping into his bones. His mind cleared a little, enough to grow concerned. "Am I going crazy?"

Shaun shook his head. "Sorry if I seem a little short but I've explained what's wrong five times already. I'm not sure you're going to remember whatever I say so it's difficult to get excited about sharing this again. But in the hopes six is the charm, here goes. It's Thursday. You were—"

"What?" Tad exclaimed. "Missy and I did the set-up on Monday before we got stuck in the cabin."

Shaun raised a brow. "Well done. First time you've been able to remember that without prompting. You remember anything else you did with Missy?" Tad swore and Shaun pumped his arm into the air. "All right, it seems we are getting somewhere. I know it drives your poor little human sensitivities wild, but I'm going to speak plain wolf for a bit. You began FirstMate with her and for some stupid, idiotic reason you stopped. You can't stop a trigger in mid-pull, Tad. All you've managed to do is get the bullet in motion and you've hit a time warp. Until you finish what you started, neither you nor Missy will be able to touch another person without pain. That's number one. Number two is none of us knew Missy is an Omega wolf and—"

"A what?" The pain in his body faded slightly as he remembered being in the cabin with Missy. How he'd almost decided to trap her forever.

"Omega. Instead of dealing with the authority and leadership of the pack like the Alpha and Beta, she helps set the emotional track. She knows what needs to happen by instinct. Packs without an Omega often have wolves go feral or head into the illegal side of things. You don't even know they are there if they do their job right."

Tad scrubbed his hand over his face. "Is Missy okay? Where is she?"

Shaun held up a hand. "In a minute. First I need to tell you something else."

"Damn it, Shaun, you've already told me I'm not only an ass for fooling around with Missy, I'm also responsible for messing up the pack. What other bomb do you feel the need to drop?"

His friend leaned forward in his chair, eyes serious, lips pressed together. "You haven't messed up our pack. Missy is visiting and I haven't been able to convince her to tell me where she's from."

Tad shook his head in confusion. "She told me."

"Well, she must have trusted you more than you realized.

Keil couldn't even get it out of her and that tells me she's either damn strong or damn scared about something. I also never called you an ass for fooling around with Missy but for stopping. Big difference, bucko. I need to ask you something. If Missy wasn't a wolf would you have liked to make love with her?"

What was Shaun up to? "Of course. You know I've liked her since high school and I didn't know she was a wolf. I had even decided that—"

Shaun held up his hand and jumped in. "Right. Let me get this straight. You would go out with Missy, even sleep with her as a human. What if she fell in love with you? Do you think you could have fallen in love with her?"

Tad didn't understand where this was going. "Yes."

"Then you won't be upset to find out she didn't care if FirstMate triggered a false mate because she's always been a little in love with you and she figured it was far better to love you even if you didn't return her feelings." Shaun dropped his voice, shaking his head slightly. "She's hurting bad right now, Tad. She's in physical pain because of the damn trigger thing, but emotional pain too because you managed to turn her down."

"Because I didn't want to hurt her!"

Shaun pulled a face. "Well nice going on that one, Einstein. She saved your butt and she needs you. Now you can get all human shy and shit on your own time, but if you're any kind of man you're going to go and make things right with her whether she's your mate or not."

A crash carried from the kitchen into the bedroom followed by loud cursing. Shaun leapt to his feet and stomped to the door. "Bloody idiot, TJ, you burning the house down or making coffee?" He looked back at Tad. "Well?"

He was glad his brain wasn't physically spinning anymore because it was doing triple lutz trying to keep up with this conversation. "Well what?"

"Do I go get Missy or do you stay an asshole?"

He's got to be kidding. Tad gestured to the bed and his shaky body. "You want me to seduce the woman when I've been sick in bed for three days?"

Shaun laugh was harsh and loud in the quiet room. "You were over the flu the first day. The rest of it is a side effect from your own stupidity. As soon as I bring Missy in here you'll feel much better. Trust me."

Did Missy really need him that much? If Tad were thinking more clearly in the first place, he wouldn't have caused this trouble. It came down to doing the right thing.

Tad stared out the window. So much of the past couple of years for him had revolved around the pack and learning about being a wolf. He'd become so distracted by his need to become triggered, he'd left all his human goals behind. That had been a mistake.

He thought about the way Missy had grinned at him the first day they'd met so many years ago. The way her eyes lit with mischief when she'd teased him. The sound of her laughter. The touch of her hand. He caught himself smiling as he remembered how she made him feel about himself, like he was capable and trustworthy.

Holy crap, he was in love with her.

Tad took a deep breath as he realized he not only knew the right thing to do but that he wanted to do it. Longed for it. Even though Missy was getting a false-mate sign, he would make sure she never felt unloved. Really, it was no different than what his life plan had been before he'd found out he had wolf genes—meet a girl, fall in love, get married.

He turned back to face Shaun. "Where is she?"

"She's in Shaun's bed," TJ said as he stuck his head into the room and anger streaked through Tad. Shaun caught a glimpse of it and shoved TJ into the wall.

"Smooth move, slick. Tad, it's okay. I've been sleeping on your couch and one of the girls from the pack has been taking care of Missy. I haven't touched her."

TJ chuckled. "Yeah, no one touches her because it's freaky to hear the noises she makes."

"TJ!"

Tad made up his mind. "Shaun, I need to ask a big favour. Can I use your apartment for...well, until we don't need it anymore? I'll go over there. That way no one will have to touch Missy."

Shaun let out a big breath. "Good decision, Tad. See, this is why I'm your friend. Can I help you?"

Tad reached to pull on his jeans then changed his mind. He wasn't planning on being dressed for too long anyway. He gingerly slipped on the huge robe Robyn had given him for Christmas with *Pilots Do It on the Fly* embroidered on the back, and headed for the bathroom. "Give me a couple minutes to clean up. I can walk but you're going to have to drive. If I got pulled over I wouldn't know how to explain to the RCMP why I'm dressed like this in February."

"Doesn't anyone want a drink?" TJ asked as he held up the steaming pot of dark liquid.

Tad sniffed the air. "TJ, where did you get the coffee grounds?"

TJ pointed to a container on the windowsill.

Shaun coughed. "I shouldn't drink any of it. Right, Tad?"

"Right. Unless you're looking to develop strong foliage and bright green leaves."

TJ sniffed the pot. "I thought it smelt exotic..."

Chapter Eight

The sound of hushed voices faded away behind the much louder sound of her heart pounding as blood rushed past her ears. Missy pulled herself upright and stared at the door of the bedroom.

Was he really here?

The door swung open and Missy bit back a small cry as Tad shuffled into the room, his skin pale, dark circles under his eyes. His scent flowed ahead of him and washed over her like a cool breeze, and for the first time since he'd left her Missy took a full breath.

"Hey."

Her heart skipped a beat. "Hey."

They stared at each other. Missy took in every change in his breathing, every change in his expression, as he watched her for what seemed like the longest time. Just being in the same room with him eased the pain a little, the closeness filling her with the hope she wouldn't be deserted.

Then her breath caught in her throat and she gave a little sob. Maybe he was going to tell her he couldn't be with her and—

Tad stepped closer. "Missy, stop. It's going to be okay. I'm sorry. I was wrong." He was right next to the bed now. She could reach and touch him if she tried. She dropped her gaze away and clutched her fingers together.

The bed dipped as Tad sat and Missy's traitorous body leaned toward him in her need. Their shoulders brushed and the connection flared, the numbness erased from the edges inward as they touched for the first time in days. She couldn't stop the rasping breath or the tears that started to fall, and then she was in his arms and it was all right.

Not all right like when the natural wolves helped save Tad from freezing. Not all right like when she managed to find her way to the one gas station on the highway operated by wolves so she could shift and ask for help before collapsing.

All right as in he was there and he was touching her, his fingers gentle as they traced the back of her neck, pulling curls free from her ponytail. His mouth touched her cheek and kissed away the tears while he murmured his apologies against her skin, soft like rose petals.

Tad pulled back and cupped her face in his hands. He kissed her, a tender brush of his lips on hers before looking deep into her eyes.

"I had no idea."

Missy nodded. The sweet sensation of his thumb caressing her cheekbone eased her sorrow. She closed her eyes to let the comfort of being back together with her mate soothe the raw nerves, the broken pieces inside.

"Missy, I need to tell you. I mean, I want to ask you." Tad choked on his words and she flicked up her lashes to see his tear-filled eyes. The golden flecks within were larger than before as his wolf fought to rise to the surface. She smiled encouragement at him. "I don't want this only for tonight. Just for FirstMate. I'll understand if you find your real mate and need to leave someday, but I've decided if I can't have you, I don't want anyone else."

Missy scrambled to find her voice. "What are you saying, Tad?"

"I want to marry you. Not as a wolf but as a human. I know it's quick." He brushed his thumb over her lips. "I think I've been in love with you since we were teenagers. I just didn't realize it until a couple of days ago." He dropped his head to rest his cheek against hers.

Missy's heart swelled as the last of her fears disappeared. She knew they were true mates. For Tad to be willing to commit without that knowledge...

She kissed him.

Kissed his forehead and brushed her fingers over the worry lines to smooth them. Kissed his eyes, the corners of his mouth and along the firm length of his jawbone all the way to his neck. She planted small butterfly kisses up to his ear to whisper her answer.

"Yes. I love you."

He wrapped her in his arms for another moment, his torso shaking as he took an uneven breath. When he released her he was smiling.

"Good. I love you too."

Missy licked her lips.

"Oh no. That's what started this mess." Tad shook his head and covered her mouth with his hand. "I've got strict instructions about what we need to do, well, before we do anything."

Missy licked the center of his palm, let her eyes show how much she wanted him.

"You are making this hard, Missy."

"That's the idea, Tad." Missy giggled softly, her throat still raw, her body tight. But the pain eased. He was with her. He said he loved her. Her heart melted a tiny bit more.

Tad undid his robe and let it fall to the floor. He pulled off his T-shirt in one motion, and Missy stared in admiration as he stripped off his boxers to stand naked in front of her. He was thinner than most wolves, with hard, wiry muscles. A faint trail of dark curls started at his bellybutton and descended to the juncture of his legs where his cock rose, firm and erect, already weeping with desire.

"Take off your clothes, Missy," Tad said as his hand dropped to circle his erection. Missy watched, fascinated as he stroked from root to tip, a steady motion that made her knees weak. "Missy? I need you naked."

He needed her naked? Missy threw back the quilt with her hands and shoved it aside with her feet while she shimmied the oversized shirt she wore over her head and dropped it to the floor. In three seconds flat, she was naked and ready for him.

"Still no bra or panties? Hell, woman."

Missy leaned against the headboard to watch Tad prowl his way onto the bed. He crawled on his hands and knees until he knelt beside her. He picked her up and placed her on his lap, trapping her between the wall and his body.

"I'm sorry, Missy. Because I messed things up we have to—"

Missy covered his lips with her hand. "Tad, no more apologies. I love you."

He sucked her fingertips into his mouth and teased them with his tongue, his mouth hot and greedy as he took control. He kissed her, firm and demanding, his tongue sweeping without pause as need poured off him. Tad's mouth remained on hers and her hands slipped over his shoulders. She massaged the strands of muscle under her fingers, loving the way their skin sparked where they touched. She felt him stroke his erection. Brushing aside his fingers, she circled his length with her own grasp. Tad pulled away from the kiss, his head falling back as his breathing increased in tempo.

"That feels so incredible, your hands on my cock. I want to touch you too. You know that, don't you?"

"Soon. Let me help you first." He needed release before they truly started. She brought her mouth back to his, savoring the taste of him on her tongue even as she burned for the velvet steel under her fingers. She stroked, rubbing the moisture that rose to the slit of his cock over him to ease the glide of her fingers down his length again and again, until he jerked in her hand. His lips froze for a moment against her mouth. The heat of his seed washed her belly and thighs where his ejaculate landed. He whispered her name, so soft and loving, tears came to her eyes.

Missy pressed a hand on his shoulder to direct him to his back. She straddled his waist and stared him in the eyes as she traced her fingers through the semen left on her skin, rubbing it in like a fine lotion.

"Holy Toledo, Missy. The sounds you're making are killing me."

Too caught up in sensory overload she didn't realize she'd made any noise. Scent rose between them like the most exquisite perfume, flowing in streams and linking together into a new combination. She reached down and grasped his hands, kissed his knuckles, nipped at his fingers before lowering them to cup her breasts.

Tad was the one groaning as he lifted their weight in his palms. Missy smirked at the expression of sheer delight on his face. Men and breasts. Tad gazed at her with a fascination similar to the one he'd shown while admiring her truck.

But not quite. This had more adoration involved.

He touched her gently, rolled her nipples between his thumb and forefingers until they peaked, hard and sensitive. His cock rose behind her, the wet slit nudging against her backside. Tad caressed her with his strong hands, brushing in big circles and small circles until she thought she'd go mad.

Tad rolled her off, placed her on her back and dropped his head.

"I need to taste all of you, Missy." He lowered his mouth to her breast and licked. One hand snuck down to cover her mound, fingers parting her curls to slip into her sheath and circle around her clit. While his fingers continued to dance, his mouth suckled and nipped, lapping at her nipples until they were dark red against her body.

He kissed her. His mouth hot and demanding as his fingers continued to play her like a fine instrument. Every stroke, every touch, brought Missy more and more alive as the cold seeped away like a spring thaw settling over the land. The tension in her core grew higher as Tad added another finger to tease and touch. He curled around her tighter, his rigid cock pressed against her thigh, their bodies aligning and touching skin to skin.

More than the mere touch of his hands and mouth, his heartbeat and his emotions began to join with hers and connect them. Intimately. Completely. A deep connection of passions and needs, fears and hopes. It was the most intoxicating feeling, and Missy opened herself up as much as possible to enjoy the sensation. A flash of desire rolled over her and she climaxed, her sheath pulling at his fingers as he rubbed and stroked.

Tad covered her with his body, the hard head of his cock tunneling into her pussy as it continued to pulse. He watched her face as he angled his hips and pushed, his hardness gliding through her soft receptive passage. Tenderness shone in his eyes as he pressed until he was buried in her warmth, hips tight together, bodies one.

Around them the room faded until all she felt, all she saw was Tad. He was on her and in her, stretching her and filling her. He was inside her heart as he cradled her beneath him.

And then he was inside her head.

"I need you so much, Missy."

He pulled his hips back with a slow draw over her sensitive tissues. Heightened awareness of her body increased the pleasure as he sank in again. The head of his shaft seemed to swell and press harder on the walls of her core on every stroke, the heat of friction creating an inferno. Missy opened herself more, wrapped her legs around his back, squeezing to add a jolt of pressure at the base of each of his strokes.

The tempo increased and Tad thrust harder, his torso supported over her as they connected only at the hips. It felt so good, so right, but Missy wanted more.

"Touch me with your body. I want to feel every—"

"Did you just talk in my head?" Tad broke stroke and hung suspended halfway into her body. Missy protested, lifting her hips to finish the movement. She grabbed his head and pulled him down, sweeping her tongue into his mouth while she rocked her hips against him.

"Yes. Don't stop. Oh please, Tad, I need more."

He was on her like a wild thing, his body hard and touching every inch of her skin. His mouth feasted, hands dragging her closer while he sank in hard and fast. Each stroke drove her into the mattress. Missy scraped her fingernails down his back, tangling her hands in his hair as she tried to help him deeper on every pulse. The air disappeared from the room consumed by the heat of their lust. Missy cried out as her body jolted over the precipice. Tad thrust once more and stilled, joining her in release as his seed shot deep into her core and he groaned with pleasure.

Missy lost control of her emotions and a floodgate opened between them.

Every pain...erased.

Every sadness she'd felt, all her loneliness, all her fears. Washed away as Tad's strength flowed into her. His love rested on her body like a tangible object.

His frustrations of being denied releasing his wolf for so long crashed into her heart, and she reached into him and soothed the pain away. They shared without words. Their hopes, their dreams, emotions running high as they built an unbreakable connection.

Tad held her close, their bodies still entwined. The sex was fantastic but this... No one had told him his first time with another wolf would be this incredible.

"Missy?" She stroked a hand over his face. The touch was intimate and gentle, and he smiled at her. *"Does this mean what I think it means? Or is it a perk of FirstMate I was never told about?"*

Soft lips brushed his. *"It's real. I told you we were mates."*

He paused for a moment. He had a mate. He was ready to dance on the rooftops he was so excited. *"You did. I should have listened to you."*

Missy giggled. "You okay with this, Tad?"

His heart leapt. She was his and their mating was real, and Missy wanted to know if he was okay with it? *Hell, yeah.* "So far beyond 'okay' my head is spinning. I proposed to you. I meant it and now there's no way that you're ever getting away from me." Missy stroked her fingers through his hair and Tad watched the golden flecks in her eyes sparkle. It had happened. He had a mate.

Holy crap, he was going to be able to turn into a wolf.

"Exciting, isn't it Tad? You're going to be a beautiful wolf."

"How did you know what I was thinking?" While very cool this could become a trifle embarrassing if she read his every thought all the time. "And hang on, guys aren't beautiful. We're handsome or—"

"Tad. I have something I need to tell you."

Tad rolled her on top of him, needing to feel her body weight. "Hmmm. Sounds serious." He couldn't stop touching her, connecting them skin to skin.

Something clicked in Missy. It was the weirdest feeling, almost like she'd flicked a switch. He sensed her emotions shift and change from being sated and contented with their lovemaking. Tad let her crawl off him to the foot of the bed where she stared back, her big blue eyes suddenly filled with fear. He reached out, not with his hand but with the strange new awareness he'd just attained. He stroked her skin and he knew.

Everything. Holy crap, Missy was running away from the bad guys.

He shook his head hard to get his thoughts to settle back into his brain. He left the bed and scrambled through Shaun's dresser to find clothing. "Get dressed, Missy. We're going to see Keil."

Missy's eyes were huge. "I'm sorry. I never realized the danger this would put us in. I thought that if I gave you FirstMate I might register a false connection and it would make me lose my Omega skills. I didn't know we really were mates until the cabin, and afterward I was too sick to think it through." Her voice trembled and she seemed uncertain how he would react to the whole mess.

Tad scooped her back into his arms and kissed her

thoroughly, squeezing her tight. "I'm not mad at you, love. Not at all, but we could be in big trouble and we need help. Keil's the strongest Alpha in the area and we've got an in, being family and all. Now since you don't need any undies." He handed her a warm sweatshirt, kissed her nose and turned away to dress.

"I think you're an Omega as well," Missy whispered.

"Wait until we get on the road. We'll talk about it then," Tad warned.

All hell was about to break loose and there was no way Tad could deal with it alone. It was time to call in the big guns. Being a werewolf would never be boring.

If he survived until his first shift.

Chapter Nine

Tad threw his cell phone into the backseat with the rest of their things. “That’s the last chance for reception around here. We’ll have to wait until we get over the pass to try again to reach Keil.”

He glanced at Missy, noting the tension in her body as she fidgeted with the seatbelt strap. “Hey.” He waited until she looked up at him. “We’ll be fine.”

Missy nodded but it lacked conviction.

He fought to control the wide range of emotions pouring through him, some hers, some his. “Catch me up on the werewolf lessons I need. You’re an Omega and you ran away because they were nasty assholes. Right?”

Missy snorted. “You have such a way with words.”

“Yeah. Elegant and verbose, that’s me. We’re mates, but you think some jerk plans to take you as a mate anyway?”

“My brother-in-law, the Alpha. Whistler pack has gotten into illegal activities because of him. He wants to use my Omega skills. He had something on my dad years ago, which is why I ended up married to his brother. I’ve been gathering evidence to use against him with the werewolf council, but it’s tricky. It will be dangerous to attempt to bring him down because he’ll stop at nothing. He’s a skilled liar, a bully and a killer. He killed his own brother, Tad. He’s...” She turned away to stare out the window.

Tad swore under his breath. This being connected thing was brutal. Fear rolled off her and he felt every nuance to the center of his being. His need to protect her surged to overload, making it really hard to concentrate.

"Sweetheart, you've got to stop. Every time you let the Big Bad Wolf scare you, I feel the need to rip limbs off trees. It's tough enough to drive in the dark, let alone convince the border-crossing guards to allow us into Alaska, if I'm foaming at the mouth. Oh shit..."

The border. He had no ID and the Alaskan side closed at midnight. What the heck were they going to do? "So, this Omega thing? Does it give you the ability to make someone real peaceful and content so they won't look in the trunk?" Tad asked.

Missy goggled at him.

"Just planning ahead. You get to drive us through customs, sweetie. I'm going to be hiding out."

They drove in silence for a while, the dark mountains looming above the highway.

"I think you're one too, Tad. An Omega." Missy spoke quietly. She clasped his right hand, warming his fingers as she rubbed them like worry beads.

"Really?" He racked his brain for everything he knew about Omegas. Other than what Shaun had shared, it was very little. Except there was something very comfortable about the knowledge settling over him, very natural. A part of his brain he had always known was there but never used seemed newly available. "Isn't it really weird we'd end up as mates? I thought Omegas were rare."

"Mates complement each other, complete each other. There must be things that you'll be able to do that I can't, or that I can't without your help. I'm still trying to figure out the extent of my skills. I know I can calm crowds and soothe someone when they're angry. The last Omega I spoke to said he could locate pack members by their thoughts. He went through the pack each night and helped relax their burdens so they could sleep well."

Tad grunted. "I don't think being a night light is the kind of thing I'd enjoy. You really think I'm one?"

She nodded. "One of the minor skills all Omega's have is the ability to hide our scent if we need to. You were doing that even before we...you know."

"Made love? Had sex? Did the horizontal hoochie coochie? You realize we're still not done, by the way. That was nowhere near long enough or enough times for a real FirstMate. From what I've been told," Tad teased, trying to lighten the mood.

Missy kissed his knuckles. "Trust me, I'm looking forward to more as well." She laughed. "I think ours is the strangest mating I've ever heard of. It's taking the longest time to complete!"

Tad squeezed her fingers. *"I love you, Missy. And everything will be fine."*

They would be at Robyn and Keil's in an hour. Whether it was her ability as an Omega or his ability to bullshit, peace descended and Tad relaxed. It was going to work out. It had to.

He was in love and that made everything right.

✧

All the house lights were blazing as they slowed on the approach to Keil's log house on the outskirts of Haines, Alaska.

"Tad." Missy's eyes were huge in her face. "He's here."

Shit. “You sure?”

She gave him a dirty look.

“Sorry. You’re sure. Don’t worry. We’ll just go talk to him, explain we’re mates and that’s all there is to it.”

Missy turned away from him and Tad felt her fear rise again.

He, on the other hand, was getting royally pissed off. It sucked big time he’d caused so much trouble with their mating by his ignorance, but enough was enough. Werewolves or not, some things were the right thing to do. If the Alpha from Whistler didn’t understand, he could shove it up his ass.

The area in front of the house looked like a parking lot. Half the pack must have been there, and a couple of fancy rentals were noticeable front and center. Tad opened the car door for Missy and held her arm as they approached the house.

The Granite Lake Beta stepped from the shadows.

“Hell, am I glad to see you. Did you get our message?” Tad asked. Erik nodded and motioned to the side of the house with his head. Tad followed toward the edge of the stairs.

“A group from Whistler showed up today and demanded Granite Lake’s assistance in regaining one of their AWOL pack mates. They said she might be suffering from mental trauma, and they were concerned she could be a danger to others if she wasn’t dealt with properly.” Erik snorted in disbelief.

Missy clutched Tad’s arm tighter.

“Dangerous? Missy? Please, what kind of crap are they trying to pull? And last time I checked there was no such thing as going AWOL from a pack. It’s not a military membership or anything.” Tad soothed a hand down Missy’s back as he looked up into Erik’s worried face.

Erik squatted his huge body down to Missy’s level so they were eye to eye. “You’re close to the end of your time of mourning. Did you know Doug planned to take you as a partner?" She nodded and Erik cursed. "Damn, can't even claim ignorance and ask for an extension. I take it you'd prefer not to accept his proposal?"

Tad felt the wave of fear and nausea that swept over her.

"I would sooner permanently shift and go feral, but they threatened my sister."

Tad laid a hand on her shoulder and gave it a reassuring squeeze. "You're not going anywhere, Missy, and we can keep your sister safe." Tad turned to Erik. "We can keep her safe, can't we?" He stared at Erik, ready to do whatever it took to convince the Beta to help them.

Erik stood and rubbed his chin. "I have some friends in Vancouver that I could call in a favour from. But she would have to be ready to leave fast. In the meantime, it doesn't change the fact they"—he pointed with a thumb over his shoulder—"want Missy.

"We got your message that you plan on getting hitched. When they overheard the news, the Whistler pack stopped talking about recovering a missing member, and Doug informed us that you were promised to him. Keil's done what he could, but they've issued a challenge for Missy."

Tad wrapped an arm around Missy. "Nope. She's my mate, Erik. The real deal. They can't take her."

Erik shook his head. "That's what I'm trying to tell you. They can. They can take her if you're dead."

Well, that would really mess up his day.

"Bloodthirsty wolves." Tad cursed.

Erik nodded. "Not one of our better personality traits, I'll admit."

Tad took a long breath in and considered. He'd just been triggered. Next full moon was in three weeks. In that amount of time they should be able to help Missy's sister get away and he'd be able to prepare a battle plan. Figure out how to use his new skills as an Omega if he really did have them.

"Fine, I accept the challenge. Do they want to fight in Whistler or—"

Erik's face screwed up into a frown. "Tad, they want to fight here. Now."

Shit. Werewolf politics *sucked.* "But I can't shift yet. How the hell is that a fair challenge?" He was supposed to defend himself against a wolf attack tonight?

"There are rules about these things set out in the code, of course, but it seems since you've been triggered you count as a full wolf. There's nothing in there about having to wait until you actually can shift." Erik looked extremely uncomfortable. "It would be in the interest of fair play to wait, but I think Doug's comment was something like 'I want to kill the little bastard as soon as possible.' We're not talking about nice people here, Tad."

Missy crowded into his side. The connection between them flared. Images flashed through his mind—Missy accompanying Doug away, Tad left in safety—Tad groaned. While it was neat to know what she was planning, it was going to make it tough to give her surprise gifts in the future if they couldn't keep *any* secrets from each other. He turned her to face him and brushed a soft hand against her cheek, gazing into her eyes. He lowered his voice to speak quietly to her alone.

"Missy, you are not going with them. You think you can deny our mating and go be with Doug now? I don't think so."

She pressed her hand to his, her fingers cold and shaking. "If my sister is safe, I can stand it. I don't want to lose you. Just get her to safety and I'll eventually get away from Whistler."

Tad hugged her close, his lips brushing her cheek. This

time he spoke intimately through their mate connection trying to pass the emotion he felt along with the words. *"I can't let you go back. I can't stand the thought of him touching you. I'd sooner die killing him than let you return to a life that's caused you so much pain."*

Missy clung to him for a second then stared up at him with fear in her eyes. "It's a challenge. He'll turn into a wolf and kill you, and it will be all my fault." She covered her face with her hands. "I wish I'd never come back."

"You don't mean that." Tad held her close to his chest. *"I love you, and I'm so glad you came back north and found me."*

"But he's an Alpha wolf and he fights dirty."

Tad kissed her. Here she was in his arms, the most wonderful thing that had ever happened to him, and a criminal wanted to take her away from him. No bloody way. "I've got a few tricks up my sleeve. I can fight dirty myself if I have to. As far as I'm concerned, he's not entitled to a fair fight after what he's done to you, your family and your pack."

Erik cleared his throat. "If you're ready, everyone is waiting in the back."

Chapter Ten

Tad had seen pictures of gladiator fight rings before. This set-up was a little more archaic and rustic. On the right side of Keil and Robyn's backyard, the snow had been packed down into the shape of a small hockey rink. The cleared area nudged up against the trees that led out into the wilderness. Bright overhead lights turned the whole area into high noon.

"Someone afraid of the dark, Keil?" Tad called.

Erik pulled Missy with him toward the house and Tad watched as the light in her eyes dimmed. *"Missy. You get that look off your face and trust me. We need to decide where to go for a honeymoon. After we finish the job at Mount Logan. Liard Hot Springs in April?"*

"Tad, he jumps to the left."

And then silence.

Tad stared up toward the house. "Keil?"

Keil marched into the lit area and pulled Tad in for a hug. He wore his usual guiding gear of camo pants and padded vest. There was a tall, lean man by his side dressed in a suit who watched with cold eyes. "Tad. This is Heath, Beta of Whistler. He's here to ensure I explain the challenge and all the terms." Keil shot an evil look at the intruder. "He's also listening to make sure I don't impart any hints on how to win this thing. I'm sorry, but they've got traditional law on their side. I have total control over my own pack and territory, but these kind of challenges follow laws that are bigger than me. I suggested they wait until the next full moon so you'd be able to shift as well but the damn code says…"

Tad shook his head. "It's okay."

Keil made a rude noise. "It's not okay. Your sister is going to make my life miserable for not coming up with a better solution."

Tad looked around but saw nothing beyond the blinding lights. The rest of the yard and the house were dark shadows in the background. "Is Robyn watching?"

"Yes. Erik will stay with her and Missy until this is over. They're both safe for now." Keil straightened, looming large and dangerous. He made the Whistler's Beta look weak and pathetic.

Tad felt it again, a transfer of information to him from another wolf. Emotions rolled through his brain—his Alpha's desire to take over, his deep frustration—Tad swore softly. It wasn't just Missy he could read, he knew what Keil wanted as well. Holy shit, he *was* an Omega. He skimmed through the layers of information quickly until he understood enough to reassure his brother-in-law. "It's going to be all right. You've done everything possible. I know you'd take my place if you could, but that's not allowed."

Keil stepped back a pace. He shook his head at Tad in disbelief. "Shit, so you really are an Omega as well?"

Tad nodded. "Seems that way. What's the deal?"

"Doug wants Missy, so he has to fight the actual battle. He's able to shift as often as he wants. He's Alpha for a strong pack, he'll be a strong wolf. Don't underestimate him. You two are alone in the arena until one is defeated. Winner gets Missy."

"No weapons are allowed," Heath whined. "I want to check

you."

Keil glared at him. "We'd better pull Doug's teeth and claws, hadn't we? To make the contest more even?"

Heath shrugged. "Tad is welcome to bite and scratch all he wants to win the fight."

Tad stood silently while Heath patted him down. It made Tad's skin crawl. He wished he could fart at will like TJ, just to wipe the smirk off the asshole's face for a minute. He turned to Keil. "She's *my* mate. I can win this, I'm sure of it."

The tall stranger made a choking sound. "You're very confident. Shall we get ready? The challenge is to the death."

Tad got in Heath's face. "Really? Because I like 'to the pain' so much better, you know, from *The Princess Bride*? Death is short, but ugly lasts forever. Oops, you already knew that, didn't you?"

He turned his back on the two of them and swung his arms in a majestic manner toward the house. Okay, the whole situation had gotten a little out of hand and he'd like a bit of backup. Maybe what Tad had in mind wasn't strictly kosher but he'd use it only if absolutely necessary. A fight to the death against a man who'd killed his own brother? Tad needed to know that in the end Missy would be safe. As much as it made his stomach churn, he would ensure Doug either gave up or didn't leave the arena alive.

"What are you doing?" Keil asked.

"Communing with the spirits. You see as an Omega..." he glanced over his shoulder at Heath to make sure his words impacted, "...as an Omega, both Missy and I have the ability to use not only our skills, but the skills of the wolves who have fought here before."

Bullshit. He had a degree in it and right now it better work. He moved his arms with great care, praying Robyn was watching his "communing". *Come on, Robyn, pass on the message to your mate.*

Keil jerked beside him. Tad was careful not to look at his brother-in-law as he finished up his "magic waving". Heath had edged away from Tad a step or two. Good. Fear might help keep Tad alive and he really, really wanted to stay alive.

Another figure stalked naked toward them across the snowy February ground. Tad still couldn't get used to the way wolves let it all hang out, although this guy didn't seem to have much to hang.

Tad grinned up at the house. *"Missy, can I call your brother-in-law a wiener?"*

"You want to take this a little more seriously, love?"

"Cocktail size, I'm guessing."

"Tad, please…"

Keil and Heath stood between the two, forcing Doug and Tad to face each other across a distance of ten feet. Keil nodded to Tad once, then spoke to Heath. "I want to observe from the ground in wolf. You may join me."

Hell, yes, Keil had gotten the message. Now came the hard part, convincing the Beta to agree. Tad was sure it wasn't proper etiquette.

"A little encouragement right now, Missy, if you please. Heath needs to say yes." Tad concentrated on making sure positive, peaceful feelings emanated from himself and Keil. Nothing tricky happening here, la-di-dah.

Heath nodded, and the two of them stepped aside to strip off their clothes. Tad couldn't help noticing Keil was far more impressive nude than either of the Whistler wolves.

And wasn't that just *not* what he wanted to notice right now.

"You got an issue I need to know about?" Missy's thoughts laughed at him.

"Just tell my sister she's a brave woman."

"Bad boy. Please be careful, Tad. I love you so much."

He took note of where the men left the arena to be sure his backup plan was in place before facing Doug. There was still time for one last chance at solving things in a civilized manner. Tad held out his hand.

"Hi. I'm Tad. I understand we're kind of related since Missy and I mated—"

Doug growled and bared his teeth. His canines extended past his lips.

"You sure you want to do this? I mean, both Missy and I are Omegas and—"

"You're a fool. You have no idea how to use your skills, which is why I'm going to kill you now. You've spent so much of your life as a human and an unwanted half-blood, you have no idea of the power of a full-blood Alpha. You're even too sensitive to fuck a woman who is already mated. Oh yes, I know all about you. I looked into what kind—"

Tad socked him. Hard. Twice.

Someday the bad guys would realize monologues were a bad thing.

While Doug staggered back, Tad ripped off his coat and tied it in a quick knot. There were no other weapons at hand and when Doug shifted he wanted something to beat the shit out of the beast.

Tad wasn't inexperienced in fisticuffs. He had fought training bouts with his pack mates for the last two years. He was smaller than a lot of other wolves and knowing how to defend himself in a quick and vicious manner had stopped some of the in-pack ranking fights. He had also trained with some excellent Arctic games competitors. He just needed the opportunity to put that training into effect.

Doug came at him, swinging hard. He appeared soft but the danger in him rolled off in waves, his evil driving him forward. Tad was smaller and quick, and he dodged most of the blows, but enough landed that he knew he would be black and blue when it was all over.

As long as he wasn't dead.

There was no sense of time as the fight continued. Under the glaring lights there were only swinging shadows and pain. Tad dodged another murderous attack from his opponent, dancing away from all but a few strikes. Inevitably his body protested more and more. Blood clung to his lips and his legs grew weary.

"You're slowing down. No one is coming to save you," Doug taunted. He wasn't without his bruises and cuts, and he seemed surprised by the furiousness of Tad's counterattack.

Tad waited on the ground where he'd fallen after the last bone-crunching blow. The snow was kind of soft and gentle on his aching limbs, and it was nice to rest for a moment.

Besides, Doug needed to take one more step. Tad arranged his hands carefully, bending one leg under him and keeping the other loose and ready.

Then, glory be, Doug not only swaggered forward, he leaned over Tad to gloat. "You really are pathetic—"

Tad kicked him. He used the Alaskan High Kick method, pressing down into the ground with his extended arm while he forced his free foot up as hard and as fast as he could. Tad drilled the bastard right smack in the middle of his face. Okay, Tad cheated a little by not hanging on to one foot, but he figured the boys at the gym would forgive him for the slight error in technique.

Doug struck the ground four feet back from where he'd started. Blood poured from his nose and mouth, and he casually wiped his hand through it. Staring down at his bloody fingers, he cackled, a wild and maniacal sound.

"Well. I'll admit it. You're a stronger man than I am. I don't know if I would beat you if we continued for much longer." He rolled to his hands and knees, and sat back on his haunches for a minute. "It's been interesting but I've had enough playing. Missy's mine and you can die knowing I'm going to make her life hell."

Doug shifted.

His human body wasn't very impressive, but his wolf more than made up for it. Here was why the man was Alpha. He was huge. He was also a dirty brown, one of the few brown werewolves Tad had ever seen. Tad leapt to his feet, grabbed his coat and got it swinging, the heavy knot whistling through the air.

Doug lunged and Tad whirled aside, smacking the coat onto Doug's head. There was no use in bashing him anywhere else on his body with the thick fur protecting him. Besides, if Tad thumped his brains often enough the ass might get knocked unconscious.

Tad danced toward the edge of the arena, wanting something at his back. Doug could strike too far and too fast, and if Tad got stuck in the middle of the space it would be like tossing a marshmallow into a fire.

Doug's teeth snagged the coat and his claws scrambled over Tad's leg. He forced himself to remain standing on a limb that burned with pain while with the other he kicked at Doug's groin, trying to slow the monstrous beast a little. Blood dripped as they backed away from each other, Doug favouring his hind left leg, Tad limping as well.

A silly little thing caused the turning point of the fight. Tad wore the clothes he'd borrowed from Shaun's room, and they all fit loosely. Doug snapped at him, captured a pant leg in sharp teeth and shook like he had a rabbit in a death grip. The motion pulled Tad's pants over his hips and trapped his legs so he couldn't escape. Doug let go and watched with a wolfy grin as Tad scrambled backward crablike toward the very edge of the arena.

This was not the way it was supposed to happen. Dying with your pants around your ankles was a joke, for heaven's sake. Tad hesitated for a sheer second and Doug was on top of him, forcing him to the ground. Fiery darts shot through Tad's body as razor-sharp teeth fastened on his upper arm and snapped it in two. He screamed in pain and anger, watching the wolf retreat to the middle of the arena to gloat.

Sweat ran into Tad's eyes, stinging, and he gasped in air.

"It's time, sweetie."

A wash of cool flowed around him, numbing his arm and clearing his mind. Missy's touch was assuring and comforting. She was still confident he knew what he was doing.

Holy crap, he hoped he knew what he was doing.

It wouldn't be pretty but he had to try. He kicked off his shoes and dragged himself to his feet, letting his pants fall to the ground. He paced the perimeter of the arena, his gaze tracking Doug as the wolf snarled and stalked toward him. Tad leaned back on the tree nearest where Keil and Heath had left the arena and prayed the message had gotten through.

"Kill the lights now."

The lights blacked to nothing, leaving ghostly auroras on his retinas. Reaching blindly behind him, Tad slipped his good hand into Keil's vest where it had hung since the start of the challenge. It had to be there. Keil always wore the damn thing. He spun around and dropped to his knees cradling his broken arm as he held the gun procured from the vest. He heard Doug sniffing, trying to track him. It would be normal for the wolf to gain the advantage under these dark conditions.

Except Tad was an Omega.

All the anger built up from feeling Missy's fear of this man lifted Tad to the place where he would do anything to save her. He closed his eyes so he wouldn't strain to use his vision, and he opened his mind to the ability that had hovered under the surface for so much of his life. Tad reached out with his new awareness and found the emotions of his enemy.

It was like wearing infrared goggles.

Doug came toward him on silent paws. Tad stroked his mind, calming. Cooling. Doug paused in his pacing, his head swinging from side to side like he was dislodging an annoying fly.

Tad's heart rate increased. It was working. He pushed harder at his enemy, attempting to make Doug fall asleep. The wolf staggered in a circle, whining and snapping at the air. He clawed at the ground and snarled, obviously aware of what Tad was doing, but unable to overpower the Omega skills Tad appropriated from somewhere deep within.

Tad wanted the man out of Missy's life forever, yet the thought of killing another in cold blood just wasn't his way. Maybe there was too much human in him, but since Missy had mentioned the possibility of the wolf council or the human courts, it seemed there might be a better solution.

Doug rolled on the ground, his legs scrambling in the air as Tad continued to mentally overwhelm him. Suddenly Missy was there in Tad's mind as well, supporting him, aiding him. Doug was no match against their two strengths, untrained and untried as they were.

The sensation of Missy's presence grew stronger, and

across the arena Tad saw a shimmer of silvery fur in the moonlight. He couldn't believe his eyes as she bounded into the fight area. *"What are you doing? Get out of here!"*

She slowed to a walk, her wolf form so beautiful he couldn't take his gaze off her. *"I'm the cause of the fight. If he will deny the challenge, you don't have to kill him."*

She knew. Somehow she knew that he didn't want to kill, not if it could be avoided. His astonishment at the depth of the connection between them as mates rose again.

Tad turned to face Doug who lay twitching in the midst of the arena. "Do you yield? I'll let you live if you stand down the challenge for Missy."

Tad eased his control on Doug, enough to let him move slightly. The Alpha rolled to his belly and dropped his head to the ground.

"He yields!" The Whistler Beta had changed back to human and rushed out to the arena with Keil hard on his heels.

"Will he accept the council's examination of his leadership as well as give up the challenge?" Tad demanded, keeping his eyes on Doug.

The Alpha's gaze darted back and forth. Suddenly he gathered his legs under him and leapt at Missy. His body shifted to the left as his claws swung and his teeth reached to rip her throat open. Tad cried in disbelief, raised the gun and fired twice in quick succession before everything went silent.

Epilogue

Missy watched happily as her new brother-in-law hung up the phone and turned to give his wife a tender kiss. Now *that* was a neat sensation, to be able to think about a brother-in-law without getting nauseous at the same time.

"Whistler pack leadership has finally been reorganized by the council. They're trying to avoid getting human authorities involved to deal with the illegal items Missy had documented," Keil said. He wrapped his arm around Robyn, pulling her into his side. "You using a gun during a challenge has been forgiven in light of Doug's double-cross. Plus the fact you turned down the position of Alpha for Whistler means there's some archaic law in the code that gives you clemency."

Missy tucked herself in tighter to Tad where they sat on the loveseat. She exchanged contented smiles with Robyn.

"I wasn't going to let the bastard kill me because I couldn't shift yet," Tad pointed out. "I'm glad you were paying attention, Robyn, or I'd have been down there without a backup weapon. I felt like a fool waving my arms around signing like an idiot. And while the whole Omega thing is really cool, I need more practice before relying on it to save anyone's life."

"So, are you two official now?" TJ asked.

"Official what?" Tad asked, brushing a kiss against Missy's cheek. She breathed in his scent happily, comfort and satisfaction pooling around her.

She felt little queasy, but that was to be expected.

TJ paced the room, his long legs constantly on the verge of tripping. "Omegas for the Granite Lake pack. I know you're mates because, duh, I can smell that one a mile away. There's also this other weird scent that I think means—"

"TJ, I need you to go and get my bag out of the car," Missy ordered, flicking a glance at Tad to see if he'd caught that slip. *How could TJ have known?*

The young man sighed as he stepped toward the door. "Fine. I'll go. But I'll have you know it's not my fault I have a superior sense of smell. I think it's pretty rotten you're not letting me be around when you make the announce—"

"Go!" Missy rubbed her forehead. Okay, one of her new relatives still made her head spin.

"You are going to accept the position, aren't you, Tad?" Keil asked. "It's for both you and Missy. As well as being our Omegas, you can operate your pilot service out of Haines Junction or we can increase the bookings for Maximum Exposure and keep the family business roaring here in Alaska."

Missy enjoyed the sensations washing over her as Tad twirled one of her curls in his fingers, tugging her close to kiss her again.

"Well, I suppose it depends on where Missy wants to have the baby," Tad said as he squeezed his arm around her tighter.

She should have known she couldn't keep it a secret for long. "You knew! I was trying to hide the scent." She twisted around to face him, delight filling her.

Tad laughed. "It seems becoming mates with you has fixed my sense of smell. Plus, I'm an Omega. I know what's happening, even this quickly, and I want to tell you I'm pleased as punch."

Across the room Keil snorted. “You’re proud you’ve got super sperm. What did you do, knock her up the first day?”

Missy bit her lip and scrunched up her face to stop her enthusiastic nod. She caught Robyn’s eye and winked. Robyn’s shoulders shook with silent laughter.

“Of course, I think it would be great for the cousins to be raised close together, so living here in Haines might be the best,” Tad continued, staring at the ceiling as he rubbed at his chin.

A loud *thunk* rose from the corner of the room as Keil fell off the arm of the couch, his mouth gaping open. Robyn grinned at him, laid one arm on top of the other and rocked them back and forth.

“Shit,” Keil exclaimed. “Really? A baby? But I never smelt, I never...oh hell yeah.”

Tad’s hand slipped over Missy’s waist as he leaned closer to kiss her neck. Here was everything that she’d ever hoped for, longed for. A dream so long in the making had come true. She didn’t have to run away anymore, didn’t have to try to escape anything more dangerous than TJ.

She was home.

About the Author

Vivian was playing hooky the day they taught about the importance of getting a "real" job; she was hiding out at the local library rereading everything for the fifth time. Since then she's become a Jack-of-all-trades with a job-experience list only slightly smaller than the average phone book.

She's hiked, biked, canoed, kayaked and camped throughout Canada, Europe and the States, including Hawaii and Alaska. All these adventures have now become settings for her overactive muse to wander.

Vivian lives in Western Canada with her longtime sweetie, two wonderful kids and a dog that looks like a stuffed toy.

To learn more please visit http://vivianarend.com or you can send an email to Vivian at vivarend@gmail.com.

LaVergne, TN USA
16 November 2010
205142LV00002B/68/P